The Immortal Grave series
Book one:

Merlin's Heir

Scott R Hylton

Merlin's Heir
Copyright © 2013 Scott R Hylton
All rights reserved.
ISBN:1492359076
ISBN-13: 978-1492359074

To my wife, Joanie.
To my grandmother, Elaine.
To all my friends and family who supported me while
I worked on this.
Most of all to my friends in the Next Best Fiction
Author Contest 2013, who pushed me to finish this.

"The best thing for being sad," replied Merlyn, beginning to puff and blow, "is to learn something. That is the only thing that never fails. You may grow old and trembling in your anatomies, you may lie awake in the middle of the night listening to the disorder of your veins, you may miss your only love, you may see the world around you devastated by evil lunatics, or know your honor trampled in the sewers of baser minds. There is only one thing for it then – to learn. Learn why the world wags and what wags it. That is the only thing the mind can never exhaust, never alienate, never be tortured by, never fear or distrust, and never dream of regretting."
"The Sword in the Stone" - T.H. White

1

A soft light bathed the room in a warm glow, the large restaurant echoed with the sounds of distant laughter, a smooth jazz band, and small talk. Men and women wore tuxedo-like uniforms as they were serving food and refilling drinks for well-dressed customers sitting at mahogany tables and half-moon booths. Bits of shrubbery were scattered in corners and shelves that decorated the restaurant floor, giving a natural feel to the otherwise modern-looking building. One side of the room was a large windowed area, which revealed a beautiful image of a cloudless night sky overlooking the Los Angeles skyline.

A bead of sweat formed on the temple of a young man with trimmed, auburn hair. His hands shook slightly as he clutched a small black velvet-lined box.

"Jack?" The voice brought his attention back to the young woman sitting just across from him at the small round table they were seated at. She was only twenty-five, just a year younger than him. "You've been quiet almost all night."

His suit slightly tightened over his body as he got out of his chair and knelt on one knee next to the beautiful woman who sat across from him. Her long black hair blended nearly seamlessly with the silky black gown she wore on special occasions. The very moment the man's knee touched the ground, the woman blushed and covered her face. Her brown eyes welled up with tears of happiness as she had anxiously awaited this moment all night.

"This is it, isn't it? This is actually happening?"

"Yes, it is," The auburn-haired man nearly stammered trying to say the words, even though he had recited them over and over in the mirror. He hesitated before he worked up enough stamina to speak clearly.

"Debbie, you've been my best friend since we met in high school and I've loved you since we graduated."

He opened the black box to reveal a white gold ring with an infinity symbol encompassing two small diamonds. "My love, will you be Mrs. Jack McAllister?"

There was no hesitation. "YES!!"

Debbie practically leaped out of her chair and tackled him with a hug. As they embraced, they could hear applause from the people sitting at the tables all around them. After the applause faded, she kissed Jack passionately and returned to her seat. She presented her left hand as Jack took the ring out of its holster and slipped it on her finger. It was a perfect fit. Jack got up and sat down across from her again. One waiter came by to retrieve the empty plates from their table just before another female waitress brought a bottle of champagne to them, compliments of the house.

"I can't believe this; this is just as I've always imagined it would be. It's just so perfect." She stared at the ring before looking back up at Jack, the smile on her face seemed as though it would never go away.

"I know." He picked up his glass as the waitress poured the golden champagne to just an inch below the brim. "You just passed your BAR exam, I'll be finishing medical school by next year, we're set for life. Nothing can stop us."

Debbie picked up her wine glass and kept smiling as they toasted to their future and clinked. They were young and in love, a love story that was proof of a perfect relationship. As they sipped their drinks, they both envisioned their future together as husband and wife. They saw a future they had both wanted since their first kiss, and now, it was within their grasp.

"Oh, Jack... I'm so sorry..."

He turned around to respond to the mysterious

voice, "For what?" But there was no one there, only an empty table.

"What's wrong?" Debbie asked a bit concerned.

"I thought I heard someone talk to me just now. Did you hear it?"

Debbie shook her head, concerned. "Are you feeling OK?"

"Oh yeah, I'm great. I might have had too much to drink. Maybe it's best if I don't finish this." He set his champagne back on the table with a reassuring smile.

He shook his head a little, trying to shake off whatever strange influence had taken over him. In the end, he assumed someone's voice had simply echoed behind him.

After finishing their dessert, Jack stood up and took Debbie's hand. He gave her a playful twirl as they moved to the dance floor, holding each other close as they swayed back and forth, dancing to the soft music that played. Debbie laid her head on Jack's shoulder and hummed with the music. High above them in the night sky, two others were having a conversation of their own. Two winged figures watched the couple's embrace.

"It's always so much harder when the mortals are in love and happy," spoke the female dressed in a tight frayed red outfit torn in random areas. Little silver buckles held it together around her legs, arms, and chest. She turned to face her male companion with a look of disappointment.

"Why must we keep choosing mortals that are this happy?"

"That is not for us to decide my dear, we can only watch. All we can do is keep an eye on the mortals we know will make the sacrifice. The role they are going to play is for them to decide, not us."

"It still doesn't make this any easier..." The female turned back to watch them dancing. This time the male turned to face her.

"He will be your responsibility. Our orders were

specific: He is not to be taken by the Collectors at any cost, use force if necess-" Their conversation was interrupted when he looked back down and saw the couple driving off down the freeway. The male took off in a great hurry to follow them. The female stayed close behind him. Following the car was no issue to these winged people, they could out-fly a Blue Angels jet.

As the couple pulled into the driveway of a small, 70s style brick house, they both went into the house. Jack started a fire while Debbie went into the bedroom to change. Just outside the window, unseen by any mortal eyes, were the winged ones, watching them in their moment of romance.

"Is that why you're assigning him to me?" The female spoke, her eyes fixed on every aspect of Jack's face. "Because I know how to fend off the Collectors?"

"More or less. I know your track record isn't exactly a glorious one, and I know you really wanted a chance to prove yourself to Lady Uriel. Which is why, with such a high-priority subject, I know that you will stop at nothing to succeed in retrieving him."

The female turned to her companion, "So I'm to consider this a personal favor from you?"

He turned to her, "A favor, as well as a test of faith. Show me that my faith is well placed, Sparrow." With that, the male flew off with a thrust of his wings, leaving Sparrow to stay and keep watch over Jack.

2

Jack and Debbie went to bed that night still feeling euphoric after dinner, the champagne and dessert. As Jack fell asleep, his arm around his fiance, he imagined he would soon dream about the future and all it held for him. What he saw, however, was anything but comforting. He began seeing images moving quickly before his eyes. Things he didn't understand, much less recognized.

He saw a large black banner; a closer look revealed a medieval red dragon in the foreground. Next, he saw a sword lying on a grave, strange symbols emblazoned on the blade, which almost seemed to glow. Then a book, old and worn, that appeared as if it were bound using animal skin. He then saw a vision of four people as large as giants on equally large horses, wielding massive weapons as if they were riding off into a great battle. But the most striking image was one of a strange orb that seemed to resonate with an amazing power. His dream seemed to be focused on it, fixated on the resonating vibrations emanating from it.

As the orb floated in front of him, he felt as though he could reach out and touch it. He felt drawn to it, almost moving towards it, until his attention was disrupted by a voice speaking to him from his dream.

"Jack, I'm so sorry... It's time..."

He woke up instantly. The images remained with him for a few moments before they began to fade. He rubbed the sleep out of his eyes and looked over to his side to see Debbie next to him, still asleep. Not more than a few seconds later, the alarm went off, waking Debbie from her sleep as well. Rather than waking up, she rolled over towards Jack and wrapped her arm around him. It was then she noticed the sweat on his chest.

"Oh my god honey, are you getting a fever?" Now fully awake and worried, she felt his forehead.

Jack held her hand, "I'm fine, just a bad dream."

Relieved, Debbie lay on her back. "You'll still be able to bring me lunch today after court?"

"Oh, definitely. I'll be there," He said reassuringly, "Any preference?"

She thought a moment, "Maybe some Chinese... better yet, make it Thai." Jack chuckled a bit and rolled out of bed with Debbie right behind him.

After getting ready for the day, Jack drove Debbie to the courthouse, a large cement edifice built after a Masonic fashion the way many courthouses were built. As Debbie finished buttoning up her blue blazer, Jack couldn't help but notice how much she looked like a true lawyer who must have been practicing for years. She took the law quite seriously. She gave him a kiss and got out of the car to ascend the stone steps to her hearing. Halfway up, she paused to look back at Jack with a smile, a small breeze blowing her shiny jet black hair past her face. Her gorgeous brown eyes said everything: I love you.

Since it happened to be one of the few days Jack was off from classes, he stopped at a local coffee shop for breakfast and ordered a frozen cappuccino with a cream cheese muffin and sat at a small table out in the sunlight. It was a beautiful day. He could make out an artist drawing portraits on the sidewalk with chalk; not far from the artist was a vendor selling maps to tourists while a group of joggers passed by for a morning run. Voices from a local radio talk show chatting about politics and the economy floated across the street. It just seemed to be business as usual for the rest of the world. As Jack examined his watch, he noticed that it was nearing 11:30; he finished his frozen coffee and headed off to pick up lunch.

Jack parked his car in the parking garage near the courthouse and carried two boxes containing their favorite Thai dishes from a local take-out place up the stone steps and sat down. It wasn't long before the large wooden doors opened and people began to swarm out talking on cell phones as they descended the stairs around Jack. Debbie finally appeared looking pale, like she was going to throw up. Jack immediately stood up and ran to her, taking hold of her, worried.

"Baby, are you OK? You look like you just saw a ghost." Debbie looked into his eyes; hers were full of fear and she embraced him. He consoled her, "Talk to me, tell me what happened." He wrapped his arm around her side supporting her as they slowly walked down to where Jack had left lunch.

"My client was testifying against the defendant, a man we suspect with strong connections to the mafia. You know the one I told you about?"

Jack nodded.

"Well, one of my client's witnesses never showed up to testify and the defendant pulled me aside after the hearing and told me I had only one chance to drop the prosecution now. Well, I got a little... aggressive."

"You punched him or something?" Jack questioned.

"No, just told him I wouldn't rest until he's behind bars. He didn't like that at all..."

"And then what?"

"Well, he didn't exactly say it, but I think he threatened to-"

"COUNSELOR!" A man standing just off the sidewalk yelled, interrupting the conversation. He looked Italian, wearing sunglasses and a black coat. He raised a gun in their direction and everyone on those steps quickly dispersed, screaming. Jack instantly grabbed his fiance and pulled her down, shielding her. Three security guards reacted and pulled out their guns as well. Jack and Debbie both closed their eyes as they heard several gunshots. It felt as though the whole world shook and rattled and suddenly stopped. Debbie was the first to open her eyes and looked past Jack. The shooter was dead and the officers were securing the scene, calling for police response on their radios.

Jack and Debbie stood to embrace each other, and that's when he felt it. A pinch on his skin and his back heating up like it had just caught fire. Time slowed down as he watched his fiance let go of him and shock cross her face when she realized there was blood on her fingers. All sounds faded away except for Debbie's distant screaming. Jack's eyes turned to the sky and he realized he was falling. He landed on his back and his breathing slowed. He could only see his fiance now, tears streaming from her eyes and her hand on his cheek. He couldn't make out what she was saying; he could no longer hear anything. He looked into her eyes once more as the world faded and his life ended.

3

Silence. The world appeared broken and dark, the sky looked like twilight had ended and night had begun. Jack woke up abruptly, quickly getting to his feet. He was frightened by the memories of the last few seconds that had transpired. All he wanted now was to hold Debbie in his arms, but she was gone. 'How was that possible?' he thought to himself. It was then he noticed his surroundings in its entirety. Everyone was gone, the crowds, the policemen, the hit man, everybody.

Everything appeared unmoving, all time had stopped. Jack was suddenly aware of the world he was in. He was no longer alive and was trapped in nothingness. He was standing on the steps of the courthouse he barely remembered now. He was expecting to experience several sensations: the wound in his back, a breeze in the air, sadness, a noise from somewhere, the roughness of the stone. But there was nothing, no pain, no texture, no emotion. He was trapped in a purgatory that he could barely describe.

Jack found it funny how the moment he realized he was alone, he suddenly craved interaction, from anyone, anything. He called out for it, "Hello!" An echo, and then nothing. Again, "Hello?" Another echo, then silence. Jack decided to search for some form of life, of mortality. He walked down the streets; they were empty and lifeless ruins. Lights were off, stalls previously full of color were gray and dismal. Passing by a hotel pool, the water appeared unmoving, solid, no light reflecting.

How was it that everything around him was devoid of any character or emotion? It was almost as though any source of happiness or tranquility had been robbed. Everything he remembered about his surroundings was still here, but life was gone. He found himself at a small park, normally filled with the sound of children playing. Again nothing, no movement. He tried once more to call out, "HELLOOOOOOOO!" His voice echoed loudly, and as if the ground had heard him, it rumbled in response.

The earth shook and began to crack around him, Jack stumbled to his hands and knees, bracing for whatever would happen next. As the cracks grew, the world around him broke away. Trees, playgrounds, buildings all collapsed beneath him, descending into an unknown void. Everything fell away until only he and a small patch of the park remained, barely big enough to walk in a large circle. When Jack looked up, the horizon had become a clouded sky as far as the eye could see, nothing was there but he and the patch of land. After a few moments, he crawled to the edge and looked down. He saw more sky; he was floating on land surrounded by empty air with no visible bottom. Jack realized that the world he saw, the world he knew was an illusion. This was his fate, his true fate, solitude in an empty world.

Jack collapsed onto his back, suddenly feeling sorrow for the loss of all he knew and had taken advantage of. What was he to do now? His thoughts became his own once again.

"Debbie..." His voice was barely a whisper. He almost didn't hear himself speak. More emotions began to emerge; the first was anger.

"WHY DID YOU DO THIS TO ME? WHY AM I HERE? WHAT DID I DO TO DESERVE THIS?" He screamed at his unknown enemy, whoever it may be. He stood up again and surveyed what was around him, just grass, a patch of dirt and stones.

"What is this place? What am I supposed to do?.... Please tell me, I'll do whatever you want. If I'm dead, then where's my judgment? What's my purpose here? This can't be the end!" He hoped to hear an answer but still heard only silence.

"ANSWER ME!" He sat in the middle of the floating rock that was now his prison and tried to cry, but no tears emerged. He curled up into a fetal position and wished to feel something, anything other than emptiness.

"Jack.... Be patient..."

Jack looked up shocked, "What?" He stood up quickly to find his visitor.

"What did you say?" He looked all around him for the source of the voice, but again, no one.

"DON'T LEAVE ME HERE!" Jack was hysterical, but he didn't hear the voice reply.

Time became an elusive concept, he could no longer count how long he was trapped in his prison. It felt like hours turned into days, days into months. Jack felt no affliction from hunger or exhaustion, no need to eat, nor could he feel tired enough to sleep. He was aware of every second of his existence and his sentence here. He made several attempts to escape; he pleaded for help but received no response. He threw stones off the edge to find some kind of solid ground. He even went so far as to jump off the edge himself and fall to whatever ground there may be. He was dead after all, he couldn't die again. He fell for what seemed to be hours before he found solid earth. He didn't feel the impact but knew he had succeeded. He laughed as he got up, feeling triumphant at his effort. But his triumph was short lived when he surveyed his new landscape. He recognized the grass, the patch of dirt, all the stones he had thrown off the edge. It was all exactly the same. He had only managed to land right back on the same patch of floating land he started on.

"Impossible..." he said to himself. There was no way he could have fallen that far and found another prison exactly like the one he left behind. He was truly trapped.

Jack found solace only in his memories. He remembered his family, the only son of a wonderful mother who had always supported him growing up. He remembered the day he graduated with honors and a scholarship to practice medicine. His mother was so proud of him. His father, however, was a drunk who had never supported Jack even once, and he resented the man for it.

No attempt of escape ever worked. Jack felt he was losing his sanity, lying there on the earth as time went on. He kept thinking about Debbie, trying to imagine all of the memories he had left behind as if he could will them into existence. He remembered the first time he met Debbie. They were only friends at first, in high school. Debbie was dating someone else at the time, but they still spent a lot of time together studying. When Debbie's boyfriend broke up with her, Jack was there to console her and the two of them had always been together ever since. All he could think about now was how much he wanted to look deep into her eyes, yet now he could barely imagine them. He tried to imagine looking into Debbie's eyes and seeing them say 'I love you.'

He didn't even notice when his spirit began to sink into the shallow ground. He was too late to fight the ensnarement he now felt around him. His consciousness was fading, but he welcomed it, at last, he could sleep. As his prison disappeared from him, the last thing he heard was the only familiar voice left.

"Jack... It's time..."

And he was gone...

4

Jack's first sensation in what felt like years was his first breath of air. He saw nothing but darkness and rolled around looking for something he could visually make out. There was nothing but darkness, yet even in all this, he could tell where he was. He felt around him and found nothing but close walls and uncomfortable cushions. He was in a box, one designed for him; he was in his coffin.

Before he could comprehend how he was able to feel everything, to experience mortality again, his first instinct was to find a way out. He groaned as he pushed at the lid with both hands but it barely gave, too much weight was on top of it. He brought his knees up to his chest and pressed them against the top, using his full upper body strength, to push with his knees as the lid cracked and broke above him. Dirt began to pour over him as he clawed through it. He kept spitting it out of his mouth and nose as his feet got under him and he pushed himself up. He could no longer breathe as he pushed his arms up out of the ground and felt the cool air and the brush of grass. With all the strength he had left, he grabbed hold of the surface and pulled himself out, grasping at the fresh grass as his only leverage.

As his head emerged from the earth that was his grave, he inhaled deeply, frantically pulling himself out of the hole he had created. Once he was successful, he lay on his back and continued to breathe, savored the cool air. But he winced as he heard all the noises around him, the birds, ambulance sirens, car horns honking. He heard the world as if hearing it for the first time. It was as beautiful to him as it was painful. After a moment, the noise quieted and calmed, and Jack relaxed.

He looked around with a million questions running

through his mind: Was this another illusion? Why could he now feel? Why did he wake up in his grave? At second glance, he noticed he was wearing his favorite suit. It made sense he would be wearing it now, his mother would want him to wear it for his burial.

Confusion flooded his mind and finally, he saw something he was sure was an illusion. Sitting on a large monolithic tombstone was what appeared to be a woman with wings, the span of which was unlike any other creature in the world. She wore a tattered red outfit with a hood over her head. She sat with one leg up to her chest, her other leg hanging over the edge, slowly swinging back and forth, like she'd been waiting there for a very long time. The moment Jack noticed her, she spoke to him.

"Well it's about time, I was beginning to wonder if I was watching the wrong grave." The mysterious woman jumped off the tombstone and hovered briefly just before her feet touched the ground. She wore no shoes but instead had foot wraps that matched the red material her dress was made from.

Jack scurried backward away from the stranger. "Who are you?" he asked nervously, not sure if he could believe what he was seeing.

"Calm down, I'm not here to hurt you. Yes, I'm real, and no, you're not dead." Her words cut him deeply, it was almost too much to believe. How could he not be dead after what he had suffered? "My name is Sparrow, I'm a Watcher. I was sent here to watch over you until you could be retrieved."

"Retrieved? What the hell does that mean?" He stood up, struggling a bit after all the effort he had used to get out of the hole. Seemed like he was asking a lot of questions for someone who was supposedly dead.

"You've been chosen to become an Immortal, one of the Chosen." She started to approach him.

"Don't come near me!" Jack got defensive like a cornered animal, lashing out at anything that came near him.

"Calm down! I'm trying to-" She was interrupted by what sounded like a guttural moaning and the grinding of bones. They both looked in the direction of the noise to see two horrendous-looking creatures. They resembled beasts like wolves but were more of a random collection of various bones than a skeleton. They crept up like hunters, ready to make their kill. The next few moments happened quickly, but a lot took place in that time. In mere seconds, Sparrow had grabbed Jack and taken off in amazingly quick flight. The beasts took off towards them, their speed nearly matching the winged woman. They sped down the busy streets, the beasts climbing buildings trying to keep up with the ascending woman. One of the beasts pounced at them but Sparrow twisted away from it and the beast fell. Sparrow flew straight up into the sky and the second beast leaped up to grab them but was struck down as Sparrow bludgeoned the beast with a wing.

By the time Jack realized what was going on, the battle was already over. The winged woman dropped him off at the top of the nearest building. Jack stumbled the moment his feet touched the ground. He felt like he was going to throw up, but he had nothing in his stomach. "Yeah, I'm going to need a minute." He held himself up with his hands on the ground, but they were still shaking, he felt so dizzy from the ordeal.

"Fair enough." She sat down on the edge of the building. "I think I took care of those collectors anyway." She looked over the edge, satisfied with her work.

"Collectors?" He was almost able to stand now. She turned back to him, her face still mostly hidden by her hood. Jack thought it was rather odd that she should hide her face regardless of her massive wingspan.

"Bone Collectors. They watch over people they suspect to be Chosen, like you, and when those people emerge, they kill them and take their bones for their city."

"What city?" Jack felt like himself again, whatever

that meant now.

Sparrow was about to answer, then hesitated, like she had said too much already, and instead changed the subject. "We should get moving, lots of business to attend to." She stood up, ready to leave.

"No! I'm not going anywhere else with you until you give me some answers! What do you want with me?"

"I'm trying to protect you!" she shouted, removing her hood. It was then that Jack saw her face fully. She had shoulder-length blonde hair that was full and a little curly; it shone like woven gold. Her eyes were a brilliant green and her skin was fair and smooth. There was no way something like her could be an illusion.

He froze as he gazed upon her. "You're an Angel..."

"Oh, you just noticed?" She put her hands on her hips and feigned surprise.

Jack felt like blushing. "Sorry, I just didn't think..."

"Yes, I know, no need to say it. We're already used to it." She obviously had this conversation before. "So are you ready to go then?"

"Well... How do I know for sure that this isn't all just another illusion that will disappear soon?"

Sparrow raised an eyebrow at him, "You need more proof than me?"

Jack reluctantly nodded.

"All right, come with me and I'll prove it." She extended her hand.

Jack had no idea what was going on. If he were dead, this illusion would disappear soon anyway. If he truly were alive again, she could be the only person able to explain what the hell was going on. Jack decided to trust her for now as he took her hand. They both flew off.

5

"Seriously? One of the billions served every day?" Jack couldn't believe the Angel's choice of undeniable proof of his returned mortality was the most recognized fast food chain in the world. They had landed in an alley just around the corner from the restaurant. As soon as Jack was set down, they walked towards the entrance. Somehow those yellow arches had a very sobering effect on Jack, just seeing the people going through the drive-thru, all the people working in there, the food they ate like it was just another day as usual. None of them were aware of how much they were taking for granted. Once your life is over, you can't enjoy anything anymore, you begin to miss the little things like a good cheeseburger. Speaking of which...

"I didn't realize how much I missed this."

"Then let's go eat," Sparrow replied.

Jack liked the idea, but a thought crossed his mind. "Do Angels eat?... Can I eat?" His eyebrows furled in confusion. The implications of someone who was once dead, much less not of this world, would ever get hungry was quite astounding.

Sparrow giggled in response, "Immortals like us can eat, but it's not vital to our existence like those mortals inside. We're free to enjoy the food, but we won't ever perish of starvation if we don't."

"OK, but what about your, uh..." Jack motioned his hands like wings. Sparrow full out laughed at the comment.

"Don't worry, mortals always only see what they believe to be true, nothing more. I can walk in looking like a normal human, and so will you."

Jack nodded and realized what she just said. "'So will I'? What does that mean? You're saying I look different?" Jack made a quick inspection of his body, as far as he could tell, he looked exactly as he did before he died, aside from the dirt on his suit.

The two of them walked inside the building; surprisingly, no one gave them any strange looks, no snickers or looks of surprise. Jack quickly walked into the bathroom to see what Sparrow had meant. He looked at himself in the mirror when he noticed the difference she was referring to. He looked exactly the same as he did before except for one detail: His eyes. His irises were now red, the color of his eyes had gone from his normal brown to a strange red. He leaned in to see them more closely, it almost seemed like a natural color aside from the way they glowed a little. Like he was a possessed victim in a horror movie.

Jack returned to the dining area of the restaurant to find his Angel friend sitting in a corner booth with a tray of food. He sat across from her and practically melted from the wonderful aroma of the french fries in front of him.

"Dig in." Sparrow sounded so casual about it.

"Red eyes? Is this a normal thing?" Jack was terrified, but it didn't stop him from opening the cardboard box containing a large burger, picking it up and examining it. It appeared real enough.

"Absolutely, every Immortal that is reborn bears the eyes. It's what allows them to see what truly exists." Sparrow crossed her arms and watched out the window, trying to stay on the lookout for more collectors. Jack stopped a moment and looked at her.

"Every Immortal? There are others?" The concept hadn't even occurred to him. That he was not the only one this has happened to.

"But your eyes are green," Jack mentioned.

"I'm an Angel, not an Immortal like you."

"What's the difference?"

Sparrow sighed, "We do have a lot of similarities, but Angels are chosen specifically by the Creator. Those who have dedicated their entire lives to self-sacrifice. Let's just say that Angels have certain perks that Immortals do not."

Jack nodded, "How many others are there?" Jack took a bite from his burger eagerly and his taste buds were suddenly overcome with the flavor. The meat was savory, the lettuce and tomato were crisp and juicy. Overall, the burger tasted amazing, more so than he ever imagined. He realized how much the sheer flavor had meant to him, he almost didn't hear what Sparrow said next.

"A lot actually, though a mere fraction compared to the population here in the mortal realm. Only those who died selflessly protecting someone are selected to become one of the Chosen. They're held in Purgatory until they are needed." She looked back at Jack who didn't take his eyes off the sandwich in his hands.

Jack couldn't help but shed a tear before he spoke, "How long have I been gone?" His voice was low, a sorrowful whisper.

Sparrow couldn't help but feel pity as she replied, "Umm... about four months by my count. Which is a lot longer than average. I'm sorry, I didn't mean to sound condescending when you awoke."

"Four months?" Jack looked up to meet her eyes, ignoring the apology, "That's it? It felt like almost a decade!"

Sparrow was silent to his response and looked out the window again. Jack was appalled by this information and wasn't sure how to react.

"If I'm Immortal, does that mean I can't die?" The thought of it intrigued Jack.

"Well, yes and no. You won't ever age and you won't starve. But if you suffer a large enough wound, you can still die."

As Jack attempted to understand the situation he was in, a thought occurred to him. If all of this was real and he was back in the world of the living... "I want to see Debbie." He began to slide out his booth, wanting to run straight back to his house but was stopped by one of Sparrows wings blocking the end of the booth.

"That's the last thing you need to do right now, as far as she knows, you're dead. It's forbidden!"

"Says you." He tried pushing past her wings, but they felt as solid as steel. He kept pushing, but they wouldn't give.

Sparrow said nothing for a moment until she turned her head as if she heard a noise. Her face changed and she scooted out of the booth herself. "We have to go now." She grabbed Jack by the arm and practically dragged him out, leaving the food on the table, Jack grabbed a few french fries and ate them as he was pulled away from what now seemed like heavenly food. As soon as they reached the door and went outside, Sparrow surveyed the surroundings.

"Why the hell am I forbidden to see her? She's my fiance!" Jack was very annoyed that he had to be led like a dog on a leash.

Not turning to look at him, Sparrow replied, "She was your fiance, just like you were alive. You can't go back to your past, even if you tried. Just like in that restaurant, everyone you knew, including her, wouldn't see you even if they looked straight at you. It's a terrible fate, I know, but all you can do now is move on. Now let's go."

Sparrow grabbed Jack's shoulders from behind him and they took off into the air; the initial velocity nearly whiplashed Jack. He hated the fact that he couldn't have another chance to see his girlfriend, but it seemed that he didn't have a choice now, Sparrow wasn't going to let him out of her sight. They sped off north at incredible speed, passing clouds and flocks of birds; the moon shone brilliantly above them compared to the dimming glare of city lights below. They passed over large fields of vineyards and other farmland before a large mountain came into view. Sparrow made a beeline for that mountain and before long, they were right over the crater at the top, and Sparrow descended.

"Where are we?" Jack looked around and saw nothing but the stone crater that surrounded them.

"We're at the root chakra of the earth, but mortals know this place as Mount Shasta," Sparrow explained. As they reached the ground within the crater, Sparrow set him down safely.

"Root Chakra? Are you saying this place is magical or something? It's just rocks and..."

As Sparrow approached the stone wall, they began to move and open like a big maw, revealing a passageway into the mountain. The spectacle shocked Jack. Sparrow turned to him motioning him to enter. "Let's go."

Jack hesitated for a moment, unsure if he could still believe his eyes, then walked inside with Sparrow. The maw then closed behind them.

6

"I can't see a thing." Jack walked blindly in the darkness with his hands stretched out in front of him, trying to feel his way around the dark; he took small steps through the dark corridor for a few feet before he was met with a bright light. A large double door had been opened by Sparrow revealing a room lit to expose all of its dimensions, but no light source could be seen. Jack examined the room: the walls were covered in a myriad of dials made from some combination of brass and stone. Each dial could be turned to different settings, each setting marked with strange symbols Jack had never seen before. They were unlike any manner of script ever seen before by the human race. On the opposite side of the room was a large circular edifice which looked like it was made of the same material as the dials. Just a large ring with just a blank stone wall inside of it.

"What is this place?" Jack was struck with a combination of wonder, amazement, and awe.

"Well... I guess you could say it's a kind of portal." She walked towards the dials and turned them to different settings.

"So how does it work?"

"Look, I could tell you, but we're on a tight schedule as it is. Basically, you set the dials to a certain combination and you can travel to just about anywhere." She kept turning dials as she spoke.

"OK, then where are we going?" As he finished the sentence, the symbols on the dials lit up and the circular edifice spouted open in an aetheric glow. The edifice was really a gateway and shone with a brilliant blue inside the ring.

"Now the gate closes behind whoever enters, so we

need to go in at the same time." Sparrow's voice quickened as she stood next to him at the doorway. She wrapped her arms around Jack and whether or not he was ready to step inside, she pulled him into the doorway where he was met with an extremely versatile turbulence like he was inside a tornado. The feeling was only momentary and he found himself briefly on his feet again before collapsing. His stomach turned and he felt like he was going to throw up again.

"... I'm going to need a minute."

"There's no time, just walk it off." Sparrow picked him up by his arm and as Jack raised his head, he got his first look at his new surroundings. They weren't in the small stone room anymore. Although the dials and edifice were still around them, they were in a large open area that was filled with light. Looking around them, Jack saw several Angels flying around ahead.

Two enormous obelisk-like towers were on either side of them, both as creamy white as the purest ivory. Large window-like openings dotted its sides for entry and exit like two large pigeon coops. The sky was cloudless with no sun; the light seemed to come from everywhere in the sky. The ground was made of what looked like a pure white stone. Everything about this place was so white it was almost impossible to see in this place.

As they walked through the center, Jack couldn't stop looking up at the towers. "What is this place? Heaven?"

"Close enough," Sparrow replied, still holding Jack's arm. "This is the White Gate, the most glorious kingdom in the universe," she spoke with pride. As they approached the towers, she led them towards the left structure. Jack regained his composure and gestured to Sparrow that he could walk fine.

"I thought you said I wasn't dead? Why am I here?"

"You're not; one of our oldest and most respected Angels wishes to speak with you personally."

Jack was taken aback by the comment, but couldn't help feeling like he was getting special treatment. When they entered the tower, Jack looked up and saw that it wasn't a traditional tower. Rather than being built with several floors divided into even more rooms, the tower was open all the way to the top. Platforms peppered the walls like large roosts; Angels could be seen ascending and descending to different levels. Jack almost chuckled to himself at the apparent similarities between this place and a large birdhouse. Sparrow stopped him at the center of the room and turned to him, brushing off the dirt left on his suit and straightening his collar and sleeves.

"Now, when you're presented, you are to kneel first and address him as 'Lord Azrael' or 'Sire' only. Speak when spoken to, and give him nothing less than respect."

"Azrael?" Jack recalled the name from his bible study when he was young, but remembered him mentioned as being the Angel of Death. Why did Azrael want to see him, he wondered.

Sparrow's green eyes met his. "Lord Azrael," she clarified. Jack nodded and Sparrow lifted him by his arms again as she flew upwards into the tower. As they ascended, Jack saw each of the levels and the activities taking place. Some looked like classrooms, others looked more like libraries, and several more looked like common rooms and barracks. They reached the top to find the largest room just under the pinnacle of the obelisk. A large ornate room filled with bookshelves filled to the limit with old tomes surrounded by stacks of even more books. On one wall was a large opening with another Angel standing in front of it. He looked old, but his robes were ornate and decorated, his wings were much larger than Sparrow's and looked as aged as he did. His presence just emanated with wisdom and righteousness.

As Sparrow set him on the floor of the room, she stood next to him and knelt down before the Angel. Jack, on the other hand, awed by the Angel, forgot to kneel until he felt Sparrow pull his arm down, then dropped to one knee as well.

"Lord Azrael," Sparrow spoke first, "I've brought the Immortal as you commanded."

Azrael approached her, his kind and wise eyes fixed on Jack, "Were you met by any Collectors?"

"Two, but I intercepted and evaded their pursuit. Nothing I couldn't handle."

Azrael placed his hand on Sparrow's shoulder and smiled at her, "It seems my faith in you was very well placed then. You have my gratitude." Sparrow didn't respond to his remark, no reply, not even returning his smile. The Archangel approached Jack now, "Rise, Jack." Jack stood up and met his eyes; they were a very peaceful blue. He then saw the Angel's hair was long, going past his shoulders, and white. Not a pure white, but aged white. Azrael examined him a moment.

"You look quite dirty, Jack." He smiled as he spoke, he had a comforting voice, like what you would expect from a grandfather. Jack looked down at himself and remembered he was still wearing the suit his mother had buried him in and it was still covered in dirt from his grave. He looked back up at the Archangel and hesitated before he replied.

"I-I'm sorry, I didn't have time to change..... Sire." His voice was low, almost scared.

Azrael chuckled, "It is no problem, I have a gift for you." He motioned to the table near his side, where Jack saw a set of clothes neatly folded and stacked on it. The clothes themselves were white, but there was another set of straps and hard black leather coverings that went with it. These weren't just clothes, it was armor. Next to the table was a dressing screen where he could stand behind to change his clothes.

Jack slowly approached the table, picked up the clothes, and walked behind the screen. He removed his suit and as soon as he hung it over the top of the screen, it was immediately taken away from the other side, followed by a woman's voice he hadn't heard before, "I'll have these cleaned and returned to you." The white clothes felt like finely woven cotton and were just as soft. The black leather armor was held together with straps and once he fit his head between the back and chest piece, the rest of it seemed pretty self-explanatory. It wasn't very elaborate, only covering the essential parts: chest, back, elbows, knees, and feet. When he was satisfied that it fit right, he emerged from behind the wall and met Azrael's gaze. The Angel had a look of pride on his face.

"That armor suits you, Jack, fitting for an Immortal of your stature."

Jack was confused by his comment, just as much as why he needed armor, but thanked him all the same.

"Sparrow, will you take Jack to the Forum before resuming your duties?"

"Yes, my lord." Sparrow bowed to Azrael before leading Jack to the opening they entered from. Sparrow took hold of Jack once more and they descended the tower. Jack thought back on the encounter and he just had to ask, "Why did he want to see me?"

"Who knows? He has his reasons." As they floated down with Sparrows wings, all Jack could do was wonder why he was so special. Why would an Archangel request him specifically? Why was he given these clothes? As they reached the bottom, Sparrow led him back to the portal they arrived from. As she began turning dials, Jack stopped her a moment. "What's the Forum, exactly?"

"Sparrow paused, her hand still on one of the dials. She brushed away her golden curls and faced him. "It's basically a place separate from here where Immortals like yourself find their calling. You can have opportunities to practice a craft and learn to make yourself useful. You'll also find the living quarters there; your room's already been picked out."

"So... It's like a University?"

"Exactly." As she spoke, she turned the dial her hand was resting upon and the portal opened. Jack's stomach turned a bit, remembering how he felt the last time he walked through this portal.

"Have fun." Her voice was teasing and without another word, she pushed Jack through the portal into the turbulence.

7

Jack found himself on his feet again and felt the familiar sickness in his stomach, though not as bad this time. He might even get used to the turbulence in time. He took only a minute to compose himself before looking around. Jack was shocked, thinking 'Was this the Forum?' It looked more like a Renaissance festival. The whole place looked like a medieval town filled with bustling crowds, a large marketplace lined the streets. Large ornate pillars held up buildings and provided cover for various craftsmen. As he walked down the streets, he saw dozens of shops selling hand-made clothes, weapons, trinkets, furniture, various objects he'd never seen before. In a large area that looked like a town square, performers could be seen surrounded by large groups of people watching the spectacles being performed: acrobats, stacking themselves on each others' arms and shoulders, bands playing, and a fire dancer who looked as though he could control fire itself without needing a pole or poi ball to swing it from. Those who weren't performing or watching the performances carried baskets of food or bundles of materials to other shop owners and craftsmen.

Something else he noticed was the looks he was getting from the people. Although it was true they were all Immortals like him and all had red eyes like his, they still looked at him like he was out of place. Everyone treated him like he was sick or radioactive, keeping their distance from him. As he stood apart from the crowd and the square, he found himself next to what looked like a blacksmith forge. Inside were a dozen men and women working with steel and other metals to create tools, weapons, and other crafts.

One of the blacksmiths near him was hammering a

blade on an anvil when he noticed Jack standing there. The blacksmith was tall and olive-skinned, covered in soot. His black hair was short and he had an athletic build. He plunged the blade in the water bath and steam billowed. The blacksmith then approached Jack and presented him with the unfinished blade. Jack took it but was a little confused at his gesture.

"You're not worried I might steal it and run?"

The olive-skinned man chuckled, "You must be new here." He took the unfinished blade back and placed it on a rack. "Did you want to see--"

Then it happened. All in the blink of an eye, a large explosion erupted from inside the forge itself. Jack was momentarily unconscious and awoke seconds later in the middle of the square. Crowds were frantically running to escape the chaos caused by the blaze that was consuming what was left of the forge. Jack examined his body, he wasn't hurt, just knocked down by the blast. The same could not be said about the others caught in the blast. Jack stood up in pain and checked the men who were injured. Two of them were dead, including the olive-skinned man. The others were alive but badly injured.

Recalling his training, the once medical student went to work, helping to tend to the wounds while pulling people away from the fire. More explosions began to erupt from the fire. So many people were hurt, many looked like they weren't going to make it.

"SOMEBODY HELP ME!" Jack called out to the crowd of frantic people, but nobody seemed to hear him. He found another injured person, but this one was different. He wasn't a blacksmith but wore a blue tunic and glasses on his face, a scholar perhaps. The scholar wasn't hurt, so Jack tried to wake him up, hoping he could help him. The scholar woke up and looked at Jack.

"Please, you have to help me. There are a lot of people hurt here, can you get up?" As if ignoring Jack, the scholar in blue got to his knees and checked his pockets and belt, then crawled on his knees as if searching for something. Jack implored him again, "Please, they need help!"

Jack's words seemed to fall on deaf ears; the scholar looked around as if shocked and ran off into the crowd. Jack was appalled by his reaction but went back to pulling people away from the fire.

Another man ran through the crowd and met Jack. It was one of the performers, the fire dancer.

"Are you okay?" asked the fire dancer who wore black pants and shoes with a red doublet.

"Yeah, but there are still people inside and I can't get past the fire."

"Leave that to me!"

Before Jack could stop him, the fire dancer stood and approached the blaze; he held out his arms and pulled one hand along his arm. As he did, the fire changed direction and was drawn to his hand almost like he was siphoning the fire itself. As he did, the fire became smaller and smaller. Jack watched in amazement; the fire dancer was actually consuming the blaze through his hand. When the fire was gone and no more smolders remained, the dancer ran into the building and pulled out a woman who was coughing badly and laid her down with the others.

"Anything I can do for them?" the dancer asked.

"We need to try and stop the bleeding." At his word, the dancer ripped his shirt into rags and placed pressure on a victim's wound.

The square was nearly empty now, no more help was coming and too many people were hurt and dying. Jack did all he could to help them, but it was too much. Feeling distressed over losing all these patients, Jack felt himself nearly begin to cry; he didn't want to fail, he didn't want anyone else to die. He was about to give up and run away, to find someone, anyone, who could help them instead.

Suddenly he felt a strange sensation within his hands. He observed them and his eyes grew large as they suddenly began to glow with a white light that became brighter and brighter before expanding up his arms and covering his body. He felt a strange sensation all over and it was getting stronger and stronger. The dancer, not removing pressure, watched in shock as Jack suddenly burst into a large explosion of light that covered half of the town square. When the light faded, Jack looked normal again but fell to his knees. He felt his stamina had been greatly drained.

As he looked to the dancer, looking for some sort of answer as to what had just happened, he got one. Not from the dancer, but from the victims all around him. All of them sat up and got to their feet, their wounds healed completely, showing not even a single scar. The only ones who didn't wake up were those who were dead before the light erupted. Everyone there looked at Jack with awe and approached him. Then they all fell to their knees and rained praises on him.

"Praise to you healer!"

"Thank God there was a Vigilant--"

"-- great healer."

"-- Vigilant of White Gate!"

They all surrounded him and clutched his arms, praying and weeping. Jack was afraid and wasn't sure what just happened. He broke free from the victims that had been miraculously healed and ran off into the streets. Jack needed time to think about this. What had happened to him? How did it happen? Why did they call him Vigilant? None of it made sense. He had very little stamina left, but he still made a good distance from the crowd before he ran out of breath and energy and stopped in a dark alley. Jack nearly went into shock and collapsed on the ground with his back to the wall.

"HEY!" someone called from down the street. Jack hoped it wasn't another blacksmith coming to continue their praises. His pursuer nearly missed him in the alley as he ran past and backtracked to find Jack sitting in the dirt. It was the fire dancer; he had followed Jack all the way down here.

"Hey, you OK, dude?"

Jack nodded in reply, he took a closer look at the dancer now and noticed he had short dirty-blonde hair and a slight scruff on his face. He was still shirtless and had a slightly athletic build, the kind that said he did parkour a lot.

"Good. So... what the hell happened back there?"

"I wish I knew!" Jack was frustrated; he didn't want to be hounded right now.

"OK, alright. Jeez.. Just trying to help out a Vigilant."

There it was again, that name, Vigilant. "Why is everyone calling me that?"

The dancer was genuinely surprised by Jack's response. "You don't know? How long have you been an Immortal?"

"Less than a day."

"That's weird, then why are you wearing their uniform? Well, aside from the headband that is."

"Uniform?" Jack looked down at his clothes, the pure white attire, the black leather armor. So this was a uniform?

"So what the hell are they then?" Jack wanted some answers now. No more weird illusions.

"The Vigilantes of White Gate are members of an elite group of Immortals who work directly for the Archangel Uriel. Think of them as the White Gate's personal army. Not everyone is chosen though; some Immortals spend decades trying to apply. They're highly respected as great warriors and healers, but... I've never seen one heal people en masse like you just did"

Jack was confused, "You mentioned a headband?"

"Yeah, the Vigilants receive the uniform at the start of training and get the headband to complete the uniform at the end of graduation."

"But I didn't sign up. Why would they give me a uniform? Unless..." Jack recalled his trip to see Azrael, how he felt he was receiving special treatment.

"What's your name?" Jack eventually asked, feeling like he was rude not to have asked sooner.

"Tobias." He extended his hand.

"Jack." He took the outstretched hand, shaking it.

Tobias pulled him to his feet and led him out of the alley.

"So what now?" Jack asked anxiously.

"Now? We're gonna go to my place and get you some new clothes, so no one else mistakes you for a Vigilant. Then we're gonna go help those blacksmiths clean up their shop."

"We are?"

"Yeah, it's the least you can do after running out on them like that."

8

They returned to the blast site with Jack wearing a red shirt and some jeans he had borrowed from the fire dancer and, after apologizing for not showing respect when the blacksmith guild had only shown their appreciation, explained that he was not an actual Vigilant and had no idea how he was able to heal them all at once. The blacksmiths were more understanding than Jack thought they would be. They took a moment to remember those who died at the beginning of the blast and they started repairs.

Jack was helping Tobias pick up the scattered tools when their previous conversation picked up again.

"So you were about to say something before?"

"What's that?" Jack kept his focus on locating more tools.

"You asked why they would just give you a uniform, unless..." Tobias mimicked him and motioned for an elaboration.

"Oh right, I just found it strange until I remembered that since the moment I was retrieved by one of the Angels, I felt like I was being given special treatment. Like they were making exceptions just for me," Jack looked at Tobias, his eyebrows raised.

"I'll say! Angels rarely ever go out of their way to retrieve an Immortal, much less escort them to the White Gate. If you ask me, it's pretty obvious they know something about you that you don't even know. And they want to do anything they can to persuade you into being on their side."

Jack laughed at the comment, "So what, you're saying I'm special now? I mean look at you Mr. I-can-control-fire-and-suck-it-up-with-my-hands."

It was Tobias's turn to laugh at the comment now,

"Believe what you want, but manipulating fire is actually pretty common for your average Immortal."

Jack stopped a moment and stood up, his arms full of metal tools, "Seriously?"

Tobias nodded, "Why do you think I work as a street performer? For kicks? There's not a very big market for guys like me, I have to do what I can." As he spoke, they walked back to the forge and set the tools on the table. The head blacksmith thanked them and let them know that they had done enough and could leave.

"Sorry, I didn't mean to-"

"It's OK," Tobias interrupted, "I know what it's like to be thrown into this new world. It sucks balls.... What's that?"

Jack looked in the direction Tobias was looking, "What's what?" They were looking under the table behind one of the legs and saw a small piece of cloth sticking out. Jack knelt down to grab it; it was a small satchel. Jack opened it and emptied the only object inside into his hand. It was a small crystal ball no bigger than a tennis ball. But the moment it touched Jack's skin, he was suddenly stricken with visions of death, demons, a woman screaming, and a familiar man in a blue tunic smiling as he held the same crystal ball. The sheer weight of these visions caused Jack to lose balance and drop the crystal ball. Jack fell with it, but the visions stopped the moment it left his hand. Tobias helped him up and reached for the crystal ball. "NO, DON'T—"

But Tobias had already touched it and was just fine. It seemed that the crystal didn't react to him at all. Sensing that something was wrong, Tobias grabbed the satchel and placed the crystal ball back inside before handing it back to Jack.

"You should probably hold onto it until we figure out what it is."

Jack agreed and placed it in his pocket. He was getting tired of feeling sick in his stomach and falling over all the time. Tobias helped him to his feet and brushed off the dirt.

"Is there anything to do around here that won't make me pass out?" Jack half-jokingly asked.

His friend patted him on the shoulder. "How about some entertainment?" he replied with a smile.

Jack was curious. "What do you have for entertainment? Seems a little too old-fashioned here."

Tobias chuckled under his breath, "I think I might know something you'd like."

Tobias led him outside of town through some old streets. It seemed that the further they walked, the more decrepit the buildings along the roads became. It was like crossing the railroad tracks to the bad side of town. After a few minutes, Tobias had led him to a district filled with warehouses. They walked around to a door in the back of one warehouse that appeared to be an employee's entrance. They entered to find the place stacked with large wooden crates filled with who-knows-what inside them. Along walls and scattered in different areas were shelves that had trade goods not held in crates: weapons and armor, sacks of grain and salt, baskets of fruits and vegetables.

They traveled through the warehouse like two mice in a maze of crates. There were employees around the building, hoisting crates with pulleys and chains. They gave Jack strange looks but made no attempt to stop the two from trespassing. 'What is this place?' Jack wondered. After navigating around for a minute, Tobias came upon a small staircase that led to a red wooden door. The fire dancer turned the knob and entered as if he'd been there many times before.

As Jack followed him in, he was met with a dimly lit hall. A large roar could be heard from somewhere within. More stairs descended into darkness before being met with a hallway lit by oil lamps along the walls. They were underneath the warehouse; what lay there was a mystery to Jack. But if it was as much fun as Tobias made it sound, it was at least worth a look. They reached the main room as well as the source of the noise. It was a fairly large room filled with men and women standing around a ring divided by a banister in the center.

Tobias led Jack through the crowd and motioned towards what was apparently a very large hole leading deeper into the earth. As he looked down into it, he saw what appeared to be an old mining tunnel. The walls glistened with strange crystals that reflected and magnified the lamplight, giving a clear view of the tunnel's interior. But there was a much more momentous distraction.

Jack's eyes were drawn to the pair of people within the tunnel. The two of them fought fiercely, brandishing weapons and using strange powers to push each other away and defend themselves. As Jack watched the two fight amid the crowd's screaming and cheering, the room's purpose was clear. He turned to Tobias, shouting over the crowd.

"An arena? Is this to the death?" Jack was astonished by how barbaric this 'fun' turned out to be.

Tobias smiled and placed a hand on Jack's shoulder. "It's against the rules! You can't kill your opponent, just force them into submission!" Tobias shouted just as loud. The crowd's cheering was like a long, solid roar. As Jack looked down to watch the two combatants fight it out, he noticed that although they were fighting fiercely, neither of them seemed intent on killing the other. It was almost like watching the mixed martial arts fights on TV, only these combatants were able to use weapons and had strange powers to boot.

After a couple minutes, one of them was knocked to his back with his opponent's knife held to his neck. The crowd's cheers became louder as some celebrated his victory while others groaned at the loss of the other. When Jack turned around to find Tobias, he was no longer standing next to him, but on the other side of the room talking to a man who appeared somewhat wealthy, probably a bookie. He saw them both smile and nod, after which Tobias made his way to a nearby staircase and descended into the cavern below. He had entered himself as a combatant and, upon realizing this, Jack leaned over the banister to watch his new friend compete.

Somewhere between the stairs and the ring, Tobias's shirt had apparently come off and a shirtless and fit-looking body emerged, facing another Immortal with darker skin and a much more muscular body. A nervous fear suddenly clenched Jack's stomach. Tobias put up his arms, readying himself for the fight. The bell rang and the match began. The first one to move was the dark-skinned man, whose skin seemed to change to a strange black, steely texture. Jack thought to himself, 'did his skin just harden?' and the opponent rushed in with a large swing of his right arm. Tobias managed to roll out of the way and countered with a blast of fire from his hands. It didn't seem to harm the steely man, as though his body was impervious to harm. The opponent spun around with his left arm, connecting with Tobias and knocking him clear across the arena. Tobias got up quickly, clutching his chest as he struggled to breathe. He seemed enraged and released a much larger blast of fire, nearly setting the whole place on fire.

The blaze seemed to get smaller and more concentrated on the steel-skinned man. Before anyone else knew it, the opponent raised his arms as if to concede. Tobias stopped his flames and all that could be seen now was the steely man smoking as his hard skin had apparently become too hot for him. The crowd went wild when they saw the fire-manipulator had won the match. The two combatants went back up the stairs and Jack could see the large, dark-skinned man handing something to Tobias. Upon receiving it, the fire dancer immediately ran over to Jack and handed the item to him.

"Here," his friend presented him with a large purple orb, about the size of a grapefruit.

"What is it?" Jack asked as he peered into the orb where he could see what looked like a human figure crouched down with his arms covering his head.

"It used to have some complicated name a long time ago. Nowadays, we just call them power orbs."

"And how do you use it?" Jack examined it further; there was no obvious use for it.

"All you really need to do is hold it with both hands and try to pass some amount of energy through it, any kind will do. Close your eyes and imagine water running through your arms like pipes."

Jack did as he said and closed his eyes. He imagined the water passing through his arms like a hose, but he didn't feel anything. After a minute, Jack gave up, feeling somewhat stupid. As he opened his eyes, the first thing he noticed was that the orb was perfectly clear. Shocked, he looked back up at his friend.

"See? You did it. Easy, huh?" his friend commented.

"That's amazing!" Jack replied, "What do I do now?"

Before Tobias could tell him as much Jack felt as though he only needed to strike the same pose as the figure that was once inside the Orb. Without needing further instruction, Jack crouched down and covered his head with his arms. To his surprise, Jack was encased in a purple bubble. It was some sort of shielding power. Satisfied with his new power, Jack stood up and the bubble dispersed.

Meanwhile, the roar of the crowd had suddenly changed. Men were practically throwing themselves over the banister, leaning far over to get a good look down below. Jack found himself pressed against the banister looking down with the rest of them. 'What was so damn important?' Jack thought to himself. A pair of doors that Jack hadn't noticed before from within the cavern had opened and a figure could be seen inside. The mysterious figure was insubstantial except for a bottle of beer being raised, chugged and set down again. A combatant emerged from the opposite side of the arena and readied himself. He was also shirtless, wore a green headband, and looked like he had been an MMA fighter in his previous life. The mysterious figure finally emerged from the doorway and it was not what Jack had expected.

It was a woman, dressed in a sexy black leather outfit that was tight on her body. She was fit, but not muscular; her hair seemed dark with light golden brown highlights and grew past her shoulders. Her skin was a deep caramel color and she had what appeared to be two mirrored spider tattoos on her chest and cleavage. She was gorgeous, but the most dominating feature she had was that nearly half of her outfit was covered in an array of small knives in varying shapes, designs and styles.

"Who is that?" Jack's jaw gaped a little as his eyes locked onto her.

"That's Gabriella, the Dark Mistress of the arena," Tobias introduced her adoringly as if she were royalty. "She just showed up one day and just started winning matches, one-by-one, and she's never lost!"

Just then, the match began and Gabriella disappeared. Confused, Jack looked all over the cavern, but no trace of her could be found. The opponent, however, did not look surprised but seemed to be bracing himself. A small flash of dark blue light appeared out the corner of the cavern and a small knife suddenly flew towards the man and cut his skin. Wincing in pain, the man began to swing wildly behind him, then turned in another direction and attempted a haymaker, but again, hit nothing. More knives appeared from more dark blue flashes of light from all around the room, all of them slicing and cutting his skin until he was shaking from the pain and the obvious fear that struck him. One larger flash flew across the arena and the Dark Mistress re-appeared in full view, kicked him in the back and, as her opponent fell to the ground, climbed on him jabbing one knee into his back and holding yet another knife to his neck. Jack was horrified as he thought she was about to slit his throat, but the crowd started cheering again when she backed away from her opponent. She had won;

there was no reason to hurt him further. Jack exhaled in relief and almost jumped when Tobias patted his back.

"You okay, Jack?" He showed obvious concern.

"Yeah, just--"

"Don't worry about her, she was never gonna kill him. That's not her style."

"What does that mean?" Jack furrowed his brows.

"She's adept in the shadow arts, and even though they usually work as assassins, Gabriella doesn't. For whatever reason, she just wants to be a combatant." A smile of respect crossed his face, "I think she's just in it for the glory."

Tobias watched her as she casually strolled through the doors. It was almost as though there was more than adoration in Tobias's eyes.

"You like her?" Jack joked as he nudged him with his elbow.

"It's just the way she moves, the way her butt shakes when she walks. It just makes me...." Tobias shivered and as he did, small flames erupted all over his arms and back, as if he had momentarily lost control. Jack just laughed and leaned forward, resting his arms on the banister. Tobias was right, this was exactly what he needed.

9

The fun was short-lived. A large rumble like a train passing through was heard throughout the room and dozens of men and women brandishing weapons and wearing the familiar white and black uniforms flooded the room and surrounded the crowd. A woman wearing the same uniform then entered and inspected the terrified group of spectators. She had a very commanding stature that complemented her brilliant platinum hair. As she came into view, one other feature came into view, wings. It was another Angel, but not like the others Jack had met earlier today.

"I ask that everyone here form two lines and empty your pockets when asked. When you're cleared, you may leave. If anyone shows any restraint, I will snuff it out and you will be dragged out. Thank you for your cooperation."

This Angel means business, Jack thought. He recognized the uniforms they wore, the same uniform that Azrael had given Jack when he arrived at White Gate, but they also wore a white headband with a silver plate attached to it. So these were the Vigilants of White Gate, it seemed. What were they looking for, he wondered. What was so important that such drastic measures had to be taken? His hand brushed against his pocket and he remembered the crystal he had found earlier and the effect it had on him when it touched his hand. Could that be it? A nervous feeling washed over him and he stood in line as everyone was being inspected; the seriousness on the Vigilants faces said they would strike anyone who even flinched suspiciously. The line moved slowly, but the suspense was beginning to make Jack sweat. There were only two other people ahead of him being inspected and he was next. After they were cleared, Jack stepped up and tried to remain calm before the fierce-looking warrior.

"Lift your arms out to your sides," the Vigilant commanded. Jack did so and the warrior patted him down; Jack knew the warrior had felt the satchel in his pocket.

"Empty your pockets."

Once again, Jack did as he was told, pulled the satchel out and held it in view.

"Empty the satchel into your hand."

Jack hesitated; he didn't want to see those images again.

"Empty your satchel into your hand. I won't ask again!"

The warrior placed his hand on his weapon, Jack looked to his side and saw that the angel was watching him with silvery eyes. Since Jack couldn't do anything else, he opened the satchel, and turned it upside down over his hand and watched the crystal orb land in his palm. The whole room seemed to slow down; the Vigilant's eyes widened and his companions surrounded him. The visions came back again, more clearly this time; Jack saw demons laughing, a large castle floating above a desolate desert, a woman screaming as she burned. The world slowed down even more and everything started to turn black as Jack descended into darkness again. Jack dreamed for the first time in what felt like a decade. He saw all that he had seen before. The large banner bearing the symbol of a medieval red dragon, the sword with emblazoned symbols lying on the grave, the old book bound with animal skin, the giants on horseback riding to battle, and the strange orb which his dream focused on. The very same crystal orb he had found on the ground not so long ago.

10

Jack woke up in a haze, his vision blurred at first and then blinded by a white light. He heard a voice as he lifted his head.

"I hope you don't mind that I put you on the floor. We don't sleep, so we have no need for beds."

Jack's vision came into focus and he saw the source of the voice. It was the Angel that had come into the arena, so commanding then, so serious. Yet now she seemed sincere and kind, more angelic. But Jack didn't let down his guard; he remembered what had happened with the orb and tried to stand.

"Where am I?" Jack felt like he was waking up from a deep sleep.

"My quarters in White Gate. Let me introduce myself first." The Angel approached Jack and extended her hand to help him up, then held on it to shake his hand.

"I am the Angel Uriel, Commander of the Vigilantes of White Gate." Her voice was much sweeter than before, like the soft sound of a harp. Jack looked around and saw a few other Vigilants guarding the room, then looked back at the Angel.

"I'm Jack--"

"McAllister, yes, I was briefed on who you are. I was told you were retrieved only yesterday and have not had much time to adapt to your new life." She turned and walked to a table in the middle of the room with an ornate wooden box and opened it. "Which is why I'm curious as to how you came into possession of this." She held the crystal orb in front of her and looked at Jack with a questioning glance.

Jack felt like he could trust her with the truth.

"I just found it."

"Where?"

Merlin's Heir

"At the Forum, actually, next to the blacksmith's guild, not long after an accidental explosion."

"You were there during the explosion?" Her voice was full of concern, then changed to questioning again. "I had heard rumors of a man who happened to be nearby and miraculously healed everyone who was injured, and all at the same time, if what I hear is true." Uriel placed the orb back in the box and approached Jack. "Was that you?"

Jack nodded, unsure of what all this meant, but he had a feeling he was going to find out soon enough. It was about time though; the thought of what had happened was burning a hole in his memory.

"What happened to me? What was that light? And what the hell is that orb?" The questions just flew from his mouth.

Uriel looked at him for a moment then responded. "It means that Azrael's hopes for you were well placed. The light you saw was your own body's energy, manifested into a healing light. A rare gift among Immortals, but rarer still for it to emerge at such an early stage in your Awakening. As for this orb..." She paused like she was recollecting something. Then looked back at Jack. "How much do you know of your ancestry?"

Again, Jack furrowed his brow, bewildered, but answered as honestly as he could.

"Not much really, just that I came from Scottish and English descent."

"That's all?"

"That's all I know."

Uriel's eyes turned downward; she knew something. "How much do you know about Merlin, Jack?"

The question took Jack by surprise. First, she asks about his heritage, now she's asking about Merlin? "What does Merlin have to do with this?"

Uriel took a deep breath, "Merlin has more to do with this than you think, Jack." She walked back to the orb and placed a finger on it. "For example, this 'orb' you're referring to once belonged to him. And it's more accurately referred to as the Eye of Merlin."

'Interesting', Jack thought. "But it still doesn't answer what that has to do with me."

"Please be patient, Jack. You may know Merlin as the magician who served under King Arthur and his knights. He's very well known among mortals for his rise to power and his many accomplishments. But little is taught about Merlin being a man. A mortal man just like anyone else."

Jack had never thought about that; in fact, how many people really did?

Uriel paced slowly around Jack as she continued. "After Arthur came to power and his kingdom found peace, Merlin finally settled down after he met a beautiful maiden who reminded him what a simple life was like. They were married and his wife gave birth to two sons. When Merlin died, we had hoped he would join us in his next life, but he chose to allow his life to end instead. We had hoped to have his power on our side; instead, we focused on his sons. Knowing that his heirs would carry the same latent power their father had, we watched them carefully.

"Much to our disappointment, neither of them made the sacrifice to become Immortal. We continued to watch their family lines, hoping someone with his power would make the sacrifice, but no one ever did. Unfortunately, the older of the son's family line seems to have disappeared entirely. We continued to watch the younger son's line for centuries, when one day, the day we had expected for so long arrived. Azrael had foreseen the sacrifice of the last remaining descendant who still possessed Merlin's inherited magic."

Even before Uriel finished, Jack had begun to put the pieces together. He had known that he was a person of interest to Azrael, but there was no way that he was that important!

"There has to be some mistake, I can't be that

person!"

"There's no mistake, Jack. You must have noticed when you first found the Eye that it reacted to you but no one else."

Jack was beside himself, confused as to how all this was possible. "I – I don't know, what is it supposed to do?"

Uriel smiled, "Merlin used this to see the outcome of many battles. It's also what first helped Merlin foresee the birth of a good man with royal blood who would pull the sword from the stone."

"So... it lets you see the future?"

"Not just anyone, only those who have Merlin's power. You see, this Eye is, in a way, the ultimate test of your heritage. It reacted to you and you alone." Uriel placed her hands on Jack's shoulders, her hands were soft but had a firmness that conveyed authority. "Jack, there's no doubt in anyone's mind. You are Merlin's Heir."

11

Jack was frozen, his eyes locked onto Uriel's silvery blue eyes. Those eyes conveyed that there was no deception or humor in what she had just said. Uriel slowly released her grip from Jack's shoulders, took a step back, and just watched him, probably looking for some sort of response or reaction. Many of Jack's questions had been answered, but a hundred more took their place. Uriel interrupted his thoughts.

"Oh! I almost forgot to ask, who was it that retrieved you when you had your Awakening?"

"Uh – Sparrow did." Jack finally snapped back to his current situation, but his head was still buzzing. He noticed Uriel's face change.

"Sparrow? The Watcher?"

"Yeah, she mentioned that."

"I see." Uriel motioned to one of the Vigilants and he left.

Jack's eyes were drawn back to the orb, still displayed in that wooden box. "How does it work?"

"Hmm?" Uriel seemed distracted a moment then looked back at the Eye. "Oh. Well, to be honest, we're not sure. As I said, it can only be used by a descendant of Merlin. All we know is that the Eye responds to your touch."

Jack nodded, "Whenever I touch it, I see a lot of strange visions, then I lose all my energy and pass out."

"Probably because your strength is still too weak to use it. Don't worry, in time you'll have the energy to control what you see. Until then, I ask that you put this matter out of your mind. The Vigilants and I will perform a full investigation into who stole the Eye, and why."

Jack's attention shot up. "Stole it? That orb was stolen?"

"It's an important item and we went to some trouble to procure it. It's not something we would just display for everyone to see," she said, very matter-of-factly.

It was then that Jack remembered something about the explosion. "There was a man I saw when the forge blew up. He looked like some kind of scholar. He had a blue tunic and glasses. He was crawling around looking for something after I woke him up."

"Did he have round glasses?" Uriel showed some recognition in her eyes.

Jack tried to picture his face, the scholar was about Jack's age, taller than him, with pasty skin, shoulder-length black hair, and his glasses...

"Yeah, he did. Do you know who he is?"

Uriel's expression looked troubled this time as she hesitated. "…No, I'm afraid I don't. But you shouldn't worry about this anymore. I'll have someone escort you back to the Forum. Get some rest Jack, lord knows you need it." She smiled at Jack, but he knew it was fake. Jack knew right away she was lying, she knew who the man was. But why keep it a secret? "Just one more thing before you go, Jack." She approached him once more. "I hope you don't think this too presumptuous of me, but I hope that you would consider joining our ranks... as a Vigilant."

Jack hesitated, "Well...uh.."

"You don't have to decide right now. I just ask that you think about it. We could really use your ability to heal as you did before."

Jack nodded, "Okay, I'll think about it."

Uriel smiled and nodded. Jack was led out by another Vigilant who practically rushed him to the portal he had come through with Sparrow and was practically pushed into the glowing doorway. Jack landed on his feet back in the Forum, this time without so much as a dizzy feeling. When Jack looked around, it was still nighttime and hardly anyone was there.

As Jack looked around, he noticed a man sitting at

the bottom of the steps that led up to the portal. The man turned around and Jack recognized Tobias. He had been sitting there waiting for him. Tobias got up and greeted him.

"Jack! Are you okay, man? You freaked everyone out when you passed out in the arena, we all thought you might have died."

"I'm fine, just.... Well, I can't really talk about it."

Tobias was a little disappointed, "Aw, c'mon man, you can tell me.

"I just need some sleep." Jack massaged his eyes and the bridge of his nose.

"Well, where are you staying?"

Jack's eyes opened wide, he hadn't thought of that. He didn't know where he was supposed to live. Sparrow had mentioned his living quarters were here but didn't say where. He sat down on the steps by the portal and buried his face in his hands. There was so much he didn't understand about this new life. He was sitting on stone steps in the middle of the night with no home, borrowed clothes, no money or job, and now his life was intertwined with a crystal orb that belonged to Merlin that he was expected to use again. More than anything, he wanted some perspective to what he needed to do at the moment. Just a little stability was all he wanted.

Tobias took a seat next to him and patted his shoulder, "It's fine man; if nothing else, you can stay at my place until you figure out if you want to join the Vigilants or whatever."

Jack responded with a groan, "Do I have to?"

"No," Tobias responded after a moment, "You may not see it yet, but you're basically being handed a position that many of us pine after for years and years." As he spoke, Tobias pulled a rolled up paper bag out of his pocket, opened it, and set it between them. "Want some?"

Jack peered inside the bag.

"Pistachios?"

"Yeah, I love these things. They're a lot cheaper here." He took one out and cracked it open. Jacked watched him eat them for a while then decided to have a few. After what felt like ten minutes, Tobias broke the silence.

"So what did you do to end up here?"

"Huh?" Jack didn't understand his question at first.

"Your self-sacrifice, what did you do?" He popped another pistachio in his mouth.

"Oh... it was my fiance She just got started as a lawyer in L.A.; she was getting out of a hearing for some scumbag she was prosecuting when some guy with a gun just appeared out of nowhere. I can barely remember what happened next. I guess I stepped in front of her and took the bullet."

Tobias nodded, "Good man." He stared off in contemplation, so Jack had to ask.

"What about you?"

Tobias paused a moment, still staring off in front of him, "It was my brother. About ten years ago, my brother was diagnosed with severe coronary artery disease."

Jack recalled his medical training. "You would need a heart transplant for that."

"Yup, and he had a blood type that was.... well it's not extremely rare, but it's rare enough that finding a donor would take too long."

"So what did you do?" Jack ate another pistachio.

"My brother meant everything to me. I spent months watching him go from treatment to treatment, watching him struggling to breathe, the convulsions, my mother crying as she held him. I just... I couldn't watch it anymore." His eyes started to well up a bit.

"You don't have to finish man."

"No, no, I'm fine, really." Tobias regained his composure, sat up straight and continued.

"I, uh, wrote a note. Explaining that I had his blood type, left it on my nightstand, grabbed my dad's gun and...."

"You took your own life so your brother could have

your heart," Jack finished the story, knowing it would be too painful to remember. Tobias just nodded and his eyes were starting to look better. The paper bag was empty and Tobias crumpled it up and burned it in his hand. Jack leaned away from the flames a bit, and as the ashes were carried off in the wind, Jack asked something that had been on his mind for a while.

"Why are you helping me out so much? I mean, I've barely been here a day and you've given me clothes, offered your home to me, even got me that shielding power from the arena. Why?"

Tobias snickered, "I thought you were a Vigilant, I wanted to help out with the fire, it's kind of my thing, you know?"

"Well yeah, but, after you found out I wasn't a Vigilant. Why did you keep helping me?"

Tobias was at a loss for words for a moment, then answered, "Okay, to be perfectly honest, you look a lot like my brother."

That made much more sense; these people he was thrown in with weren't just everyday people. All Immortals had given their lives up for something bigger than themselves, something they believed was worth dying for. Maybe this new life Jack had wasn't as confusing as he thought it would be.

"Have you seen your brother since you got here?"

Tobias's face changed, almost looking guilty, "Uh... it's forbidden, didn't they tell you that?"

"You're lying, my fiance used to have that same look when she lied." They both laughed at the comment. "Come on, you can tell me."

The fire dancer leaned in close after a second and spoke in a hushed tone. "Okay, no one else can know, but a lot of us remember the combination to go back to the mortal realm, so sometimes we go into visit our loved ones, just to see how they're doing."

Jack spoke just as quietly, "What if they see you?"

"They don't. They believe we're dead, so they never see us. Which is really convenient, but every once in a while, they occasionally get a small glimpse of us out of the corner of their eyes; be especially careful around really little kids, cause they don't understand death."

"What do you mean?"

"Mortal people can only see what they believe; they believe we're dead and in the ground, so they can't see us. Little kids, however, don't understand that yet, so in their mind..."

"They think we're still alive."

"Exactly."

Jack had remembered when Sparrow had explained all of this to him, but not as completely as Tobias had. But Sparrow had been in such a hurry to bring him here. Maybe Jack didn't give her as much credit as she deserved. She did try to explain as much as she could with the little time she had, and perhaps, if they hadn't stopped to eat, she could have explained more to him. No wonder she looked so annoyed. As his thoughts were drawn to her, they heard the portal opening behind them. In the darkness, they saw nothing but light shining through and the silhouette of a figure walking towards them.

"Good, I don't have to hunt for you." The light from the portal faded as it closed and the figure became clear. It was Sparrow, standing there with her arms crossed, looking straight at him. Jack and Tobias stood straight up and Jack spoke first, "You were looking for me?"

"Yes," she said with a bit of a smile on her face, "I'm to be your guardian for now."

12

"My guardian?" Just when he thought the confusion was starting to clear up, more showed up.

"Yes, for the foreseeable future, I'm to watch over you and protect you from anything that might threaten our newest celebrity." She said the last part with a little condescension.

Tobias chuckled when he heard Sparrow say that. "Okay, given that the healing power he has is pretty impressive, 'celebrity' is kind of stretching it, don't you think?"

Jack was silent, but Sparrow didn't waste a second, "So you haven't told your new friend yet?"

Jack remained silent for a moment before answering, "No."

"Told me what?" Tobias was suspicious and rightly so. Jack had meant to tell him, just not yet. Sparrow beat him to the punch.

"Jack here is actually a direct descendant of Merlin himself, and even inherited his powers." Sparrow seemed a bit smug when she revealed this. "And I get to be his guardian."

Jack started getting suspicious that Sparrow was hiding something too like she had ulterior motives. He couldn't imagine what she would be up to, so he kept the thought in the back of his mind.

"Okay, so... You're going to follow me around?" Jack had never had a bodyguard; he had no idea what was supposed to happen.

"More or less. I'm to show you to your quarters, then I'll be staying with you there until the Vigilants find out more about who stole the Eye and why, and during that time, we can talk."

Talk? Jack thought. In the short time Jack had

known Sparrow, he found that she was anything but a conversationalist. But I have my own place already? When did this happen? More questions arose with every hour that passed. For the moment, he just shook off the confusion and decided he would figure it out later.

"OK, then." Jack turned to his friend. "I guess I'll meet up with you later."

"Yeah," Tobias got up, "You know where to find me if you need me." He gave a casual salute with two fingers and walked off. Jack turned back to Sparrow and motioned for her to lead the way. He followed her for about ten minutes before they arrived at one of the large buildings Jack had seen when he first arrived. It probably should have occurred to him that in a place that looked like Renaissance Italy, the larger buildings would be apartment complexes. It was elegantly built; Jack had only seen Tobias's living quarters so far, which was small, but humble.

They went inside and climbed the stairs to the second floor. As they reached the door to what must have been his living quarters, Jack's eyes widened in surprise. He had pictured something basic: a studio apartment with essentials, which he would live in until he could afford better accommodations. The apartment he received, although it was still a studio apartment, was huge! A finely-dressed bed was at the end of the room. Bookcases filled with large books lined half of one wall.

Upon closer examination, Jack saw that there were volumes about the explorations of magic, healing techniques, theology, history books on The White Gate and some place called The Abyssal Throne, books about various weapons throughout history, and mixed military tactics. A large wardrobe lined another wall. When Jack opened it, he found the suit he was wearing before coming here but cleaned and pressed. More than that, however, were many other suits from various eras in history that were tailored for distinguished members of the time, but they all appeared to be in his size.

"This place is amazing, Sparrow," Jack spoke excitedly, but in a hushed tone.

"Not bad for a Freshman dorm, eh? There's room for further decorations if you want." Sparrow seemed legitimately happy to see Jack liked his living quarters.

"All this because I'm a descendant of Merlin?" Jack was still going through his new suits in the wardrobe.

"Of course. White Gate likes to take care of their own after all; you should see what the Vigilantes have. They get great pay and better quarters up in the west tower at--"

Jack cut her off as he slammed the door to his wardrobe. He was silent for only a moment before he took a breath and spoke, "Why don't you just say it?"

"Say what?"

Jack turned to face her. "I've had suspicions all day, and then that other Angel lady, Uriel, told me she had been looking for one of Merlin's descendants to join her. And now you bring me here to this great apartment and try to tell me about the perks of being a Vigilant?" Jack was becoming more upset with every word, "Can you make it any more blatant that you're all buttering me up to join the Vigilantes? Tobias told me about that uniform Azrael gave me and said that the Forum was for Immortals to find their place and discover who they are with their new lives, but all of you are just short of yelling at me to become a Vigilant on day one!!"

"That's not true!" Sparrow almost seemed offended. "I honestly don't care one way or the other if you do, I wouldn't even be here telling you about them if I had the choice." That remark set him back a bit. Sparrow sighed and sat on a desk Jack hadn't noticed before.

"What do you mean you didn't have a choice?" Jack's voice had calmed down.

Sparrow took a moment before replying, "Here's the truth. A long time ago, I was preparing to join the Vigilants myself as an officer under Lady Uriel. It was something I aspired to since I was chosen to become an Angel."

"Chosen? I thought Angels were... I don't know, created?"

"No, Angels are chosen by the Creator after they die and return as Immortals. Azrael was one of the first. He was once a very noble and honorable Judge very near the beginning of the world. Uriel was chosen after she kept her faith and refused her arranged marriage to a demon-worshiping warlord. But as I was saying, I was chosen too. Not long before my inauguration, I started training against the demons of the Abyssal Throne, and to my own dishonor, I crossed the line and traveled to the Abyssal Throne itself. That was something that was forbidden to me until I had joined the Vigilants. When Lady Uriel found out, she demoted me to a Watcher."

"Well that doesn't seem so bad, you get to help people like me, right?" Jack tried to be supportive.

"It's not like that, we're just meant to make sure that things are operating normally in the mortal realm. You may not see it, but Watchers are the lowest people on the totem pole. For decades, I wanted a chance to redeem myself. Then Lord Azrael came to me and gave me an opportunity to do just that. Under his orders, I would retrieve you when you came up from your Awakening, and bring you here. That way, Lady Uriel would see that I could follow orders, especially when it came to matters of importance, and maybe get a chance to become a Vigilant again."

Just like that, all of Jack's questions about Sparrow were answered--her condescending attitude, her eagerness to rush him to White Gate, avoiding answering his questions. Jack couldn't help but feel sorry for her and wanted to apologize for yelling at her a few minutes ago, but the words wouldn't come out. Instead, he thought maybe he could help. "So did you get your chance?"

Sparrow looked back up at him with half a smile, her mood changing slightly. "Lady Uriel assigned me to you for the duration of the investigation for starters, but she gave me an ultimatum stating that if I could convince you to join the Vigilants, then I could talk to her about my enlistment too."

"I see, if you get a 'high-priority' person like me to join, then you can too. That seems fair." They both chuckled and, for the first time, Jack saw the possibility of their becoming friends.

After a moment, Sparrow spoke, "You don't have to decide tonight, I don't want to push you into the Vigilants, but it would mean a lot to me if you did join."

Jack finally understood why Sparrow was trying so hard to persuade him and appreciated that she had told him the whole truth.

13

Jack had spent the whole night deep in thought about the events of the last twenty-four hours. He scoured his new library-like collection of books on information about Merlin: who he was, his life, tales of his magic and any evidence of his lineage in the texts. With every turn of a page, Jack found that there was more and more truth to what Uriel had told him. He found legends and stories about the Eye as well. It told of how Merlin used the Eye to foresee the coming of a battle, an assassination attempt on his king, a coming famine. Merlin also used it to see the birth of Arthur and how he would be the only one to remove the sword from the stone.

The longer he read, the more he began to believe that this was no mistake. At daybreak, he set off from his new home with even more questions running through his mind. His new Guardian stayed right behind him, following him around like a shadow. During the night, Jack had decided that it was time to explore his new surroundings; see what was there and learn what opportunities had been presented to him. Once again, he found the Forum to be not unlike a Renaissance Festival. There were the blacksmiths, of course, but he had also met with tailors who made many beautiful outfits, the likes of some already in his closet. One of them he wore now, a simple red tunic with the sleeves cut off and brown leggings that would have been worn in the Eighteenth century, along with a leather belt that went around the waist of his shirt and black leather boots that matched.

Continuing through the square, he met many performers having the time of their lives as they breathed fire and made little puppets come to life. The tricks were simple but still brought a smile to Jack's face. Alchemists were found there as well, selling medicines and wearing strange masks that made them look like birds with long beaks. Jack was particularly interested in them, as he was studying medicine in his previous life. He examined all the strange bottles, asking about how the contents affected the body. Jack became so excited that he instinctively wanted to tell Debbie about them. And then the painful memories came back.

Jack was dead; he was not allowed to see his fiancee anymore. He turned to Sparrow, watching him like some bodyguard. Jack wanted to know if Debbie was okay. What is she up to now? he wondered. But Sparrow would never let him find out and Jack still knew too little about this place to find a way to sneak away. But there was someone else who did. Jack returned to the performers in the square and looked around. There was no sign of Tobias performing right now.

Jack looked all over, hoping to find his new friend. He went to Tobias's apartment and knocked. Luckily, he was home and answered the door.

"Jack? Wow, I wasn't expecting to see you again so soon." Tobias shook his hand and invited him in. As the door swung closed, it was stopped by Sparrow's hand and she swung it back open, obviously not wanting to let Jack out of her sight. Jack turned to her with an annoyed look.

"We're just going to talk, I'm not in any danger. Do you mind?"

Sparrow looked back at him with contempt and closed the door, remaining outside as she spoke, "Don't go anywhere without me."

Jack gave her a quick nod before the door closed completely. As it latched, Jack let out a sigh and turned back to his friend.

"Something going on?" his friend asked concerned. Jack looked back at him. "I need your help." Jack's voice was almost a whisper.

Tobias seemed intrigued. "I'm listening."

"Last night, you mentioned that you once left the

Forum and went back to see your family."

Tobias's eyes widened. He already knew what Jack was going to ask and put his hands up to stop him, "Whoa now, you can't be asking me what I think you're asking. You have a Watcher outside following you, and I don't think I need to tell you why they're called 'Watchers.' Even if you can get away from her, it won't be long before she realizes where you've gone."

"But there has to be a way, it doesn't even need to be very long. Just a couple hours outside and I'll be back. I swear." Jack was determined to see his fiance one last time.

It was Tobias who sighed this time and buried his face in his hands. Then his face changed. "I got an idea, but it's a long shot," Tobias said a bit stressed.

"I'll take it." Jack was inwardly excited, "What do we do?"

"Remember the arena?" Jack nodded in reply, "Well we need to get back there, tell her we're gonna watch a few matches. I'll tell you more there."

Jack nodded at his friend's plan and they both headed out the door. Sparrow was still waiting outside like a barricade on the door. She turned to them and spoke, "All done?"

Jack was nervous, but kept his composure, "Actually, we were thinking of hanging out together today." The two men walked past her, Jack could barely make out Sparrow muttering, "Swell."

The group walked for a few minutes through the town and out into the industrial area. Jack could see on Sparrow's face that she was becoming a bit suspicious of what they were going to do.

"Where exactly are we going?" Sparrow finally spoke up.

"To the arena. Tobias and I want to watch a few matches."

Sparrow dashed in front of Jack and stopped him. A rush of nervousness ran through Jack's stomach. He thought for sure that Sparrow knew what he was planning. The guardian looked at him with a suspicious look in her green eyes. Then she spoke, "Are you planning on competing? Because if you are, we're gonna head back right now."

Relieved, Jack slowly exhaled as he replied, "No, I promise you we're just going there to watch."

"Are you going to gamble?"

"No, we're just watching," Jack spoke reassuringly but slightly annoyed. After a moment, Sparrow nodded and stepped aside. A few moments later, they reached the warehouse where the arena was hidden. They all went inside and navigated past all the crates and shelves, just as Jack had remembered. They soon reached the staircase and Tobias stopped and looked at Sparrow.

Sparrow looked back, confused, "What?"

Tobias hesitated a moment before he spoke, "Don't you think you should wait out here? Angels normally don't frequent this place. It might make people nervous, especially after yesterday."

Jack recalled the last time he was here, almost the entire army of Vigilants had stormed the place with Uriel leading them. It would make sense that if another Angel were to enter, it would cause a lot of trouble.

"I'm not letting Jack out of my sight, Elemental," Sparrow spoke defiantly.

Jack was confused by what his guardian said. 'Elemental?' he thought.

"There's only one way in or out and I'll keep an eye on him while we're in there; you have my word." Tobias seemed sincere enough. Sparrow stood there looking at him defiantly for a few moments. She really did not want to take a chance at leaving them alone, but she also knew that her presence in there would stir up even more trouble. With a sigh, she finally gave up, "Fine, but you are responsible for him. Should something happen, I will personally hold you responsible, Elemental," she exclaimed while pointing at his chest.

Tobias nodded to her and Sparrow turned to watch the area. Tobias exhaled and put his hand on Jack's shoulder and they descended into the arena once more.

14

"That was almost too close, Jack." Tobias was breathing like he had narrowly escaped death itself. He had actually stopped a few steps in and slumped against a wall, catching his breath. Even in the darkness of the hallway, Jack could see the redness on his face.

"Are you OK?" Jack asked concerned. He thought his friend might be having a stroke.

"I'm fine." Tobias straightened up and walked down the hall again with Jack close behind him.

"So what exactly is the plan now? We're pretty much stuck here."

Tobias stood close to him and whispered, "Not as much as you may think, there's more to this arena than meets the eye. You'll see." He shot Jack a smile and led him into the large cave where the arena was held. You'd never be able to tell that this place had been ransacked just yesterday. The place was full of screaming spectators as if the previous day had never happened. Apparently, this was a die-hard sport for everyone.

The two of them traversed the bustling crowd of gamblers and drunks to the other end of the cave. In an area that looked as though it were easily ignored was an old wooden door. Tobias surveyed the area, checking for anyone who may be watching and opened the door just enough to get inside. He waved his hand to Jack, signaling him to hurry and get inside. Jack dashed in and his friend quickly shut the door behind him. He whispered, "This way," leading Jack to one side of the room.

The room itself was fairly small compared to the large opening of the arena and looked as though it were used to store boxes full of bottles of beer and liquor. So this was a storage room for the arena's bar. Tobias went to a stack of shelves sitting along a wall and started to move one side of it away from the wall. The legs of the shelves dragged noisily along the floor. Once the shelves were a few feet skewed away from the wall, Tobias motioned Jack to follow him again.

As Jack peered behind the shelves, he saw what his friend was looking for. A large crevice-like pathway had been torn into the rock and led further into the earth. It was a secret escape route from the arena, he thought. Tobias led Jack through the crevice, pulling the shelves back into place to hide their trail. The whole cavern was pitch black. Tobias summoned a small flame in his hand to provide some light as they began side-stepping through the pathway.

"Why did Sparrow call you an Elemental?" Jack whispered; his voice carried easily in the narrow passage.

"Because I am."

"Meaning?" Jack inquired.

"An Elemental is one type of Immortal with an inherent ability to control one of the elements. I control fire," Tobias elaborated.

"Interesting, seems like an incredible power to have, but you said it's really common?"

"Yeah, almost a quarter of all Immortals can control at least one element," Tobias said matter-of-factly.

Jack had to ask, "And how many Immortals can heal the way I do?"

Tobias paused a moment before answering him, "Well... healing itself is actually pretty rare. You've been to the square, seen the Alchemists there, right?"

"Yeah."

"We really don't have any other means of healing ourselves. Healthcare is just as bad here as it is on earth. Any Immortal that has any ability to heal is taken in by the Vigilants. But most of them can only heal one person at a time before losing much of their strength; the fact that you can heal an entire crowd of people at once makes you one-of-a-kind."

Jack was confused, but still had more questions, "I think I understand, but you said an Elemental is only one type of Immortal; are there other types?"

"Of course," Tobias responded as if it were common knowledge, "There are rare healers, like you. Then there are Vanguards, like the one you saw me fight in the arena, who can harden their bodies. Then the Alchemists who control matter itself. There are Hunters, those bad-asses are almost as rare as healers; they have this ability to sense things no one else can and fight some of the toughest creatures in the Abyssal Throne. But they can also turn the creatures they kill into powerful weapons as well."

That name caught Jack's attention. He remembered Sparrow mentioning going there to fight demons or something, "What's the Abyssal Throne?" As Jack asked, he found himself almost tumbling forward as the crevice they were squeezing through suddenly became a large, open area. Both of them fell over each other unexpectedly but quickly got up. Tobias conjured another flame and raised it higher to survey the new room they were in. It was a fairly large cave.

Almost circular, it seemed like the cave had no other connections to any other tunnels, other than the crevice they just came through. On the floor were symbols that seemed as though they had been burned into the ground, rather than drawn, and resembled the symbols on the dials of the portal he had come through with Sparrow only a day ago. But they were different somehow, archaic to be sure, but they were shaped differently. Jack felt as though these symbols resonated with an evil nature.

In the center of the room was an arch, not circular like the portal, but more square, similar to the arches found all over Japan. Its material seemed like wood, but more black like ebony. Stranger still was how this wooden sculpture seemed to also resemble chipped stone, apparently very old. Jack couldn't tell if the gate was formed out of some kind of petrified wood, or some other material he couldn't comprehend. Whatever the case was, this arch was unlike anything he had ever seen before, even in the partial darkness that surrounded them.

"What is this?" Jack asked with a deep curiosity.

"It's a Demon Gate," His friend responded nonchalantly, but his voice still seemed to have a sense of reverence, almost fear. "There used to be a lot of them scattered all over the world, but each one is now well-guarded by the Vigilants. They believed that there were only nine of them, but this one was never found by them. It's the secret tenth Gate."

Jack was suddenly feeling the same combination of reverence and fear. "What does it do?"

"It's a lot like the portals the Angels created that brought you here, but these differ in one key aspect: The portals can only connect from one to another using a specific 'name'."

Jack recalled that the portal Sparrow opened only did so after she had turned the dials to a specific combination of symbols, which he now figured must have been Angelic script. So the symbols on the floor of this cavern must be Demonic script.

"These gates, however," Tobias continued, "can link to anywhere you want to go, whether there's a gate there, or not. The only drawback is that these arches only go one way. In other words, we can use it to go straight to wherever your old home is, but we'll need to use the portal to get back."

Jack's stomach suddenly sunk. If he used this gate, there was a chance Sparrow would suspect something and discover their plot. But if he didn't do this now, he might never get another chance to see Debbie again. It only took him a few seconds to make his decision.

"How do we use it?" Jack said, intently.

Tobias turned to him; Jack looked back. He could tell that Tobias saw the determination in his eyes, then turned to face the gate.

"All you need to do is offer a blood sacrifice, just a drop will do, and concentrate on the exact location you want to reach."

Jack took a moment to breathe, his heart was racing. He slowly stepped across the darkened symbols on the floor. He finally approached the gate and brought his hand to his face, hesitated, then bit a small chunk of his thumb just hard enough to pierce the skin and draw blood. He held his thumb, bearing a small bead of crimson, just a couple inches from the petrified wood. He closed his eyes and imagined his home in Los Angeles, the old red bricks, the tree in the front yard near the window, the blacktop in his driveway. With every ounce of courage he could muster, he thrust his hand forward and touched the gate with his blood.

The moment the blood made contact, a large blast erupted from the gate, knocking Jack backward a few feet. As his friend helped him up, they both looked at the gate, which now burned with a blue fire. The opening within the arch, where there was once nothing, became a portal looking at his home. As he looked, he could see that the doorway was standing in the exact spot he imagined standing when he envisioned it for the gate. The fire quelled into a more steady state, making the gate seem not so dangerous anymore.

As they approached the gate, the two of them passed over the symbols, which seemed to glow with a golden aura. They stood barely a foot away from the arch, a small rush of air surrounding them. The two friends looked at each other again, seeing that they both understood what was about to happen, the risk they were about to take. Jack suddenly felt guilty. He knew he wanted this more than anything, just to see his fiance one last time. But at the same time, he hated the fact that he had to drag his only real friend into this. He could very well be risking his life right now.

"You don't have to come with me. You've done

more than enough." Jack hoped that Tobias would retreat while he could. But all his friend did was smile as he gave his answer.

"There's no way I'm letting you go alone. I gave my word I would watch over you until we got back. That means a lot more here than it does in the mortal world. Like it or not, I'm going."

Jack nodded, acknowledging the gesture his friend was making. Both of them looked into the doorway again and Tobias shouted, "Ready?"

"Oh yeah."

The two of them jumped through the doorway at once and the gate closed right behind them. The blue flames that adorned the arch faded as if they had been snuffed out, the symbols on the ground became blackened and dull again. The cavern grew quiet, darkness filling the room. The only thing that broke the tranquility of the cavern was the sound of someone hiding in the crevice. A lone witness who adjusted his round glasses as he retreated through the crevice to the arena.

15

"That was somewhat... anti-climactic." Jack stood frozen in disbelief. Rather than getting tossed around like a rag doll through the portal, he simply stepped through and was immediately met with solid ground. No risky side effects with using a Demon Gate could be seen or felt. After shaking off the shock that the Demon Gate was somehow safer to travel through than the portals he had gotten used to, he looked around to survey his surroundings. He was in the front yard of his old home, the one Debbie and he had lived in together. A rush of happiness passed over him as he felt the familiar breeze of the town, the scent of the grass and trees, and the warmth of the setting sun peeking over the earth before bidding everyone goodnight. He practically ran up the steps of his porch and reached for the doorknob, but just before he could touch it, he saw something that should not have been there and his heart sunk.

On the doorknob was a special lock with a combination wheel and a small closed compartment. It was the kind of padlock that realtors used to prevent entry into the house while they looked for buyers. Jack grabbed the padlock and felt a depression he had never felt before. He barely heard Tobias, who had moved to the edge of the street.

Jack looked at what his friend was now pointing to and saw the sign which read 'For Sale or Lease' with a large red-lettered label across it announcing 'SOLD.' Jack faced the hurtful truth: He could never go back. His entire past was gone, all of it. Jack walked over to the sign and stared at it as if it were the corpse of a dear family member whom he just discovered had died. He looked at the picture of the realtor's face posted at the top of the sign–a blonde woman who simply smiled back at Jack. He had lost the last link to his past and all he saw was the face of the person who took it away, and she was smiling at him.

"Jack!" His friend grabbed his shoulder, shaking it, trying to snap him out of it. He looked at Tobias who seemed to be in a rush. "Where does she work?"

"What?"

"Debbie! Where does she work?"

Jack had been so caught up in the loss of his home that he had completely forgotten. Debbie might have sold their home, but she was probably still working at the firm. Jack started running down the street, his friend close behind him. He reached the main road and found the bus station, just in time to catch the next bus. The two of them boarded and headed downtown to the firm where Debbie worked just before he died. Night had fallen by the time they got there.

Jack ran down the street to get to the front door, but Tobias grabbed his arm, stopping him.

"Jack, remember that you're still dead. You can't get too close to your loved ones."

Jack flailed his arms trying to break away, but Tobias kept a firm grip. It took Jack a minute, but he calmed down and nodded, acknowledging that Tobias was right. His friend let him go and they stayed about a dozen yards from the door to the firm. Jack stood there, trying to stay calm, holding back the rush of emotions that were boiling inside him, wanting to be let out.

"Are you gonna be okay?"

Jack was startled when he heard the fire dancer's voice, but he replied, "Yeah, just... nervous, I guess."

"I understand. Closure can be hard to accept, especially when the person is still alive. You know, some Immortals never leave the mortal realm. They just stay here, following the people they loved, acting as though they never died. It's kinda sad, but I can see a strange sense of serenity in it too."

Jack released a small snicker, "If you're asking if I

would choose to stay here, the answer is no."

"Are you sure?"

Jack looked at him, "I can't just keep following her around. Sooner or later, we both need to move on." The two of them were silent for a few moments. "Besides, I don't think anyone in White Gate would allow me to stay here anyway. According to them, I'm too important."

The two of them laughed a bit. At that moment, the door to the firm opened and a black figure exited the building and began walking down the street. The two of them watched for a moment. Jack watched as the figure unclipped long, black hair and saw it cascade down her back. Jack had to hold back his impulse to run up to her and kiss her.

"That's her..." Jack swallowed back his impulse to cry in happiness. The two of them followed her, keeping their distance until Debbie stopped at a coffee shop just a few minutes away. As she walked inside, they stopped just before the large windowed area. Jack suddenly found himself afraid to get any closer, close enough to see her. He leaned up against the wall next to the window and took a deep breath, holding back tears.

"Are you okay?" Tobias said softly.

Jack paused, "I don't know, I just wasn't expecting it to be this hard. I mean, I want to see her, but..."

His friend placed a hand on his shoulder consolingly, "We can always go back now."

Jack shook his head, still looking down, "No, it has to be now or never. If I don't do it, I'll regret it forever." He straightened up, took a deep breath, and nodded to Tobias, acknowledging that he was ready.

Tobias squeezed his shoulder, stopping him briefly. "Remember, she believes you're dead, so she won't be able to see you. Don't be afraid." And with that said, he released Jack's shoulder. Without turning around, Jack simply moved forward in full view of the window and looked inside.

He could see Debbie clearly. She was still as beautiful as ever. Although they hadn't married, she still wore black, clearly in full mourning for Jack. She sat staring at the table deep in thought. Jack could only imagine what she was thinking about. He reminisced all the times they had come to this same coffee shop, sharing cookies, making her laugh at his jokes, looking into each other's eyes and saying 'I love you' without ever speaking a word. It was almost too much to bear and Jack couldn't take much more.

"Jack, you should not have come here!"

Jack spun around quickly. No one was there. That familiar voice had returned, but it was different somehow. Before it had been softer, almost like a whisper. But this time it was louder and much more deliberate, like a desperate warning. He kept looking around for the source, but again, saw nothing. Jack was sure that someone was talking to him; it wasn't his mind playing tricks or echoes off a wall.

He turned around to look at Debbie again. A waitress had just arrived at her table with a hot cup of coffee. But something happened that probably shouldn't have: The waitress saw Jack standing outside the window. Jack remembered how mortals can only see what they believe to be true and the waitress didn't know he had died. The waitress then smiled at Jack and waved to him, likely seeing Jack as a potential customer and helping him feel welcome to come inside.

The worst part wasn't the waitress though, it was the moment when Debbie noticed the waitress wave and looked out the window to see who she was waving too. Jack froze as Debbie seemed to be able to focus on what the waitress was seeing, then her eyes widened with recognition. Debbie could see Jack!

"She sees me..." Jack whispered, but it still caught Tobias's attention.

"What did you say?"

"She sees me." There was a hint of excitement in Jack's voice. Tobias quickly walked towards him and casually wrapped his arm around Jack's neck, pulling him away from the window of the coffee house. Jack tried to struggle against him.

"Wait! She sees me!" The last thing Jack saw as his line of sight to her was broken, was Debbie getting out of her seat. His friend dragged him a few yards away and stopped behind a van that was conveniently parked nearby, hiding both of them behind it. Jack continued to struggle against Tobias, flailing and trying to yell out. Before he could realize what had happened, his entire body grew still in shock, his voice suddenly silent, his breathing difficult. Tobias had delivered a hard punch to Jack's solar plexus. With Jack incapacitated, Tobias peered around the corner of the van. He saw Debbie rush out the door of the cafe and stop, looking around. Tobias couldn't help but feel bad for the two of them. He could see Debbie begin to tear up as she realized that Jack wasn't really there, that she must have been seeing things. The man she thought was Jack was just some random passerby who just happened to look like him. About to cry, she wiped her tears as she turned around and walked down the street, heartbroken.

Tobias took a deep breath and turned to Jack, who was leaning against the van, clutching his middle and trying to regain his breath. Tobias embraced him. "I'm sorry I had to do that, but I was afraid this might happen."

Jack regained control of his breathing and spoke, "Afraid what would happen?"

"Some people, they just... refuse to accept that someone has died. When that happens, they can still see us." Tobias let him go and stepped back. Jack suddenly realized something.

"It happened to you too, didn't it?"

Tobias nodded, "When I went to see my family one last time, my parents couldn't see me, but my younger brother... he did."

"But why the hell did you have to punch me so hard?"

Tobias looked at him nervously, "You were letting your emotions get the better of you; I had to stop you somehow." He spoke as if he had no other choice. "Anyhow, we really should be heading back to the portal. I have some extra cash for a rental car; we should be there in a couple... Jack?"

Something had caught Jack's attention; across the street was a man standing alone, watching them. Jack looked intently at him and saw that the man wore a blue trench coat with round glasses on his face, a ball cap hiding his hair. He was dressed differently, but Jack recognized his glasses. He saw them once before, not here in the mortal realm, but in the Forum. It was the same man who seemed to be in such a hurry to find something he had dropped after the blacksmith's forge had exploded.

The moment the man with the glasses realized Jack had spotted him, he began walking away. Whoever the man with the glasses was, he was the one who had stolen the Eye from White Gate. Jack followed him, Tobias, right behind him calling out his name, but Jack knew he had to catch the man and find out who he was. When the man realized he was the one being followed, he began to run from Jack, trying to get as much distance between them as possible. Jack was determined to catch him. He kept turning around corners, swerving past groups of people. Jack followed him around another corner and suddenly stopped. He was gone! Jack looked around frantically, trying to find any sign of him, but his focus was broken abruptly when a hand suddenly clutched his shirt and pulled him to one side and he was met with a familiar voice.

"Don't you dare move!" Jack was thrown against a brick wall. He looked up to see who had grabbed him. It was Sparrow.

16

"Sparrow! Wait, I--"

"I don't want to hear it, Jack." She was livid.

"But that guy is--"

"SHUT UP!!"

Tobias finally caught up to Jack just in time to run face to face into Sparrow. She glared at Tobias. Jack saw a fury in her like he had never seen before. For a moment, he thought Sparrow might actually kill Tobias. She raised a finger at him.

"You disappoint me Elemental, I thought I could trust you with him, and you helped him escape? White Gate will know about your irresponsible and thoughtless actions, mark my words."

Tobias's face went pale as he just stood frozen with fear.

Sparrow took Jack by the arms. "Jack, I'm taking you back to the Forum." She turned back to Tobias. "You, however, can find your own way back."

Before anyone else had a chance to say anything, Sparrow had taken off into the air, taking Jack with her. Her speed was still just as fast as she was when she hurried him to the portal the first time. Jack had a few minutes to think to himself during the trip. He thought about Debbie, how she had been able to see him, came outside to find him. But the hard truth now was that Sparrow would never let him out of her sight again and he would never get another chance to see her again.

Moments later, they arrived at the crater of the mountain that hid the portal. Sparrow never let go of Jack's arm as she rushed him through the rocky opening.

"I cannot believe I was foolish enough to trust a new Immortal to go out on his own and not try to get back into the mortal realm. I thought you might have been different, Jack—more responsible, more mature, maybe. But I guess I was wrong."

They had arrived at the portal and Sparrow quickly turned the dials to the name of the Forum, wasting no time dragging Jack inside. A moment of tumbling through space later, Jack felt the solid ground of the Forum steps and walked down dizzily. It took only a few seconds to regain his focus, but by then, they had arrived at Jack's apartment. Once inside, Sparrow finally released his arm, which he rubbed because it felt sore. Sparrow took a seat on a desk and rubbed her head.

The two of them remained silent. Jack kept his head down, too ashamed to look at her. The silence continued for a few minutes until a soft noise broke that silence. It was almost too quiet to hear from the other side of the room, but Jack heard a short sob. He slowly looked up towards Sparrow, not seeing her face, but he could see her golden hair move slightly, almost bouncing. Was she crying? He watched her more closely, her hand hiding her face. 'Why would she be crying?' he thought. A moment later, he felt guilt sweep over him, of course, how stupid could he be?

Her dream of becoming a Vigilant was riding on her ability to keep guard over him. And even after revealing this to him, he still went behind her back and ran away to get to the mortal realm. He had betrayed her. He wanted to say something, to apologize, maybe try to explain, but there was nothing he could say that would undo his actions. He simply sat on his bed, sulking, thinking about how he had made things harder for himself and his closest friends. He finally thought of something to say.

"Does... does anyone else know?" Jack spoke softly, almost too nervous to ask.

Sparrow became silent for a moment, probably regaining her composure, but still not showing her face. "No... just me."

Jack nodded to himself, "That's good."

"What do you mean 'good'? How could this possibly

be a good thing?" Her head was still down, but Jack could see her wiping away tears with her hand.

"At least no one else knows that I escaped from you."

Sparrow didn't answer, but Jack got the feeling she was hiding something. Did someone else know?

"How did you know I left the Forum anyway?" Jack asked. Again, Sparrow didn't respond.

Jack's vision became blurry, his body began to go weak. He felt very ill like he was going to lose consciousness. He fell backward onto his bed, staring at the ceiling. New images began forming in front of his eyes, flashing and intermingling with what he could see. A man suddenly appeared in his mind like a vision. It was him, the man with the round glasses Jack heard him speak.

"Greetings Jack, I've been watching you for a while now. How interesting that you should be revealed as Merlin's Heir. Allow me to introduce myself. My name is Vergil." His voice sounded calm and businesslike. Jack couldn't move, couldn't speak. He experienced this sensation when he first touched the Eye like all his strength was being drained.

"I believe you came across something that rightfully belongs to me. I'm sorry it had to come to this, but it was an unforeseen consequence resulting from that explosion that knocked the satchel you found off of my belt. But all you need to know is that I want it back!" The seriousness in his voice was so strong it could be felt.

"I understand that you're being recruited to join the Vigilants, which creates a unique opportunity for me. Rather than spending more months planning how to get inside White Gate to steal the Eye once more, I feel it would be more advantageous to both of us if you were to retrieve it for me. Why is this to your advantage? Well, let me show you."

Jack's vision seemed to move around the room that looked like the inside of a warehouse; he could see almost every detail. Finally, his vision focused on a large black spot in the middle of the room. It was someone with a bag over her head. Vergil removed the bag and Jack felt an anger and fear he'd never felt in his life. It was Debbie, bound and gagged, tied to a chair.

"Tell no one of this, Jack. You have two days to bring me what's mine." Jack could see the terror in her eyes, the tears rolling down her face. The next words Vergil said rang so hard in his mind, he thought his head would explode.

"The Eye... For Debbie!"

The vision vanished instantly and Jack regained control of his body just as fast. The first thing he saw was Sparrow standing over him with her hand on his shoulder. A look of worry and concern was on her face.

"Jack! Talk to me!"

Jack sat straight up and looked around. Sweat was beading on his face. He looked up at Sparrow, wanting to tell her what just happened, but remembered Vergil's warning: 'tell no one.'

Instead, he made up an excuse. "I'm fine, really."

"You don't look fine."

"No, I am. It must have just been heat exhaustion."

Sparrow immediately got up to get a container of water to bring to him. Jack took it with a half-smile and sipped from it greedily. The ordeal had left him thirsty after all. After a few minutes recovering, Jack decided it was time to act. He stood up and walked to his closet, rummaging through the different outfits he had until he found the one he needed.

"What are you doing?" Sparrow still seemed concerned, but Jack was done with subtleties.

"Sparrow, I know I wronged you. I can't make any excuses for what I've done. So I'm just going to do the right thing." As he spoke, he began removing the red clothes he had on and dressed in a white outfit--the same white outfit that had been given to him when he first arrived at White

Gate.

"What do you mean 'the right thing'?" Sparrow was confused, especially since he was changing clothes so quickly. Jack slipped on the black leather armor that went with his white robes and buckled it tightly, then turned to face Sparrow.

"I'm joining the Vigilants."

17

"Are you serious?" Sparrow, for the first time, seemed to be at a loss for words. "I mean, I just wasn't expecting--Well... at least, not this soon."

Jack took Sparrow's hand and led her out the door this time. As they walked down the street, Jack got another glimpse of what life would be like as a Vigilant. Other Immortals began stepping out of his way, offering small bows as he passed them. The Immortals seemed to have a respect for the Vigilantes that went beyond that of a regular army. They all knew something about the Vigilantes that Jack had yet to learn. Although, when he thought about it, he had never really stopped to ask about them either.

Thinking that he should probably ask Sparrow about it, he turned to her. He noticed a completely different change in Sparrow. A few minutes ago, she was grasping his arm firmly like a parent dragging a misbehaving child, but now Jack was leading her by the hand, which was now tender, kinder, more friendly. But more than that, she was staying in step with him and she was smiling. Not the kind of smile she made when she got her way, but this one was more appreciative, more grateful. For the first time, Sparrow looked at him like a friend, not just an assignment.

As the two of them reached the portal near the edge of town, Jack stopped near its entrance. "Sparrow, before we go, I need to ask. What exactly are the Vigilantes? I mean, what are they really?"

"You mean no one told you? Not even that Elemental?"

Jack recalled the conversation he had with Tobias and hoped he was okay. "Not much, just that they were White Gate's personal army. But just now, everyone we passed by acted like I was some kind of... savior. I didn't even do anything for them, aside from helping the blacksmiths."

Sparrow looked appalled, "Didn't do much? Jack, you saved their lives. You did more for them than they could ever do for you." Sparrow crossed her arms, looking a bit disappointed that Jack had brought this up. "But putting that aside, yes, the Vigilantes are White Gate's army, but they're much more than that. They're the front-line defense for every Immortal alive here today. The armies in the mortal realm did just as much for you when you were still part of their world, but they're often written off by the public. They all had a part in your defense, even if they were only indirectly responsible. The only real difference is that every Immortal here is directly affected by the actions of the Vigilants, so they have a much deeper appreciation for the things they do."

Jack had never thought about it that way. It seemed that everywhere he looked, there were people who gave everything they had just to do the right thing. the with wondered if people back home would act differently towards those who served their country if they knew how big an impact they really made. As he thought of this, he pictured Debbie being held by that maniac, Vergil. Suddenly, he knew that becoming a Vigilant was more than just an 'advantageous' opportunity, it was his chance to do more than just play his part while others did the fighting. It was his chance to fight for everything he loved. Jack felt a sense of renewal, and maybe this was what he was destined to do all along. Maybe Azrael knew what he was doing when he presented Jack with the uniform he now wore.

Jack lowered his head as he reminded himself of what he still had to do. He had to infiltrate White Gate, then find some way to steal the Eye from Uriel's chamber. The only way to do either of them was to agree to join the Vigilants of White Gate. Jack felt a resurgence of confidence in his ability to save Debbie. He began to see himself in an all new light. He thought about the man he used to be. He had spent so much of his life holding back but now realized the only way to do what was right was to take action, stand for a cause. He took Sparrow's hand again and led her up the steps to the portal. As they reached the top, Jack once again took in the sight of the great stone circle in the center and the rows of dials on either side of them written in Angelic script. Jack motioned for Sparrow to enter the combination. She approached the dials and turned two of them, but before she adjusted the third dial, she hesitated. After a moment, Sparrow turned around to face Jack.

"Jack, are you sure this is what you want to do?"

Jack was surprised to hear this. The whole time he'd been here Jack was being pressured to join the Vigilants. Now, for the first time, Sparrow seemed to be having second thoughts. "What do you mean? I told you I need to do this."

"I understand, but are you doing this for the right reasons?" Sparrow took a few steps towards Jack, "This is something you'll have to accept for the rest of your life. It's not enough to make this decision simply because you wronged me. You have to want this because it's what you really want."

Jack stepped towards her and laid his hands on her arms. He looked into her green eyes; they weren't stern and uncaring as they were before. They looked peaceful and Jack got the impression that maybe Sparrow was regretting pushing him so hard. But he still looked right into her eyes and spoke reassuringly, "I've never been more sure of anything in my life."

Jack meant those words. Sparrow simply nodded in reply and went back to the dials without another word, albeit with a look of guilt. She turned the last dial and the portal seemed to explode with blue light the way it did before. The two of them stepped in front of the portal, and as they did, Sparrow did something Jack had never seen her do: she held Jack's hand, but did so sweetly, showing how much she really appreciated his decision. The two of them

Merlin's Heir

stepped through the portal and into White Gate.

18

Jack learned that traveling through the portals was a lot like riding a roller coaster for the first time: you don't know what to expect, you get whipped around like a stuffed doll, and you usually end up puking in the process. But eventually, you learn to lean into the turns, how to brace yourself for the tumbles, and eventually, you could get off the ride feeling pretty good. As a result, this ride through the portal felt more natural. Jack stepped through to White Gate with ease. Once again, he beheld the amazing sight of the white towers and the amazing light that shone throughout the whole area.

As Jack felt the excitement of being here, he was seriously starting to consider remaining with the Vigilants. Granted that he would be able to after this whole affair with Vergil was over.

He turned to Sparrow, "So what do I do now?"

"Well, the first thing we'll need to do is report to Lady Uriel. She instructed me to take you straight to her if you decided to enlist." With that, Sparrow stepped behind him and wrapped her arms around his chest. Her wings then opened and beat downward, lifting them up and ascended.

The first time Jack was there, he was led to the tower on the left, but now, he was taken to the tower on the right side. There were some definite differences between the towers. First, the left tower was full of Angels, this one integrated both Angels and Immortals, all wearing the same uniform he had on. And as Tobias had told him, they all wore white headbands as well.

Second, the first tower had many levels and tiers designated for business and study. But as they traveled through the interior of this tower, Jack saw rooms that looked like armories full of swords and other ornate weapons, training rooms where groups of Vigilants practiced combat. Overall, it seemed one tower was meant for war, while the other was meant for peace.

Sparrow arrived at the top of the tower and lowered Jack to solid ground. He recognized this room--it was Uriel's office, where he had been before. He looked around and spotted the table with the wooden box. It sat on the desk like a centerpiece to the entire room. Jack's vision was fixated on it as if his eyes could pierce right through its wooden shell and look straight at the orb that was contained inside, the Eye of Merlin. That orb was the only thing that stood between Debbie and him.

"It looks like Lady Uriel is away at the moment." Sparrows voice broke his fixation on the box.

Only then did Jack look around and also notice that Uriel wasn't there. "Should we wait?" Jack asked.

"You can wait, I'll go find her and tell her you're here. Just don't touch anything while I'm gone." Without waiting for Jack to reply, Sparrow flew down the tower again, leaving Jack alone in Uriel's office. Jack turned his gaze back at the wooden box, slowly stepping towards it as he did. When he got close enough, he felt the urge to open it. He knew he needed to take the orb, somehow, without alerting Uriel. Jack's hand shook as he slowly reached for the lid and lifted it.

As the light hit the orb, it shimmered with a strange glow, like it was aware of Jack's presence. Unlike when he first found it, Jack felt compelled to touch the Orb. The fear he felt then when it made him nearly go unconscious wasn't present anymore. He slowly reached out for it, his mind transfixed on his mission. He kept himself focused, determined to control the effects it had on him. His fingers touched it and the surge of images and feelings rushed over him like a train. He saw everything and everyone all at once, although most of it he didn't understand. But then he saw Debbie. She was all alone and struggling to escape, but was suddenly engulfed in flames.

Jack could hear her screaming; he could smell her flesh burning. Was that what was going to happen if Jack failed to bring the orb to Vergil? It all became too much for Jack to bear; he pulled his hand away and fell to one knee in exhaustion. The lid of the box closed by itself and Jack was near to tears. There was no fighting the truth: Jack had to steal the orb somehow or Debbie was going to die!

"You're still not ready for it." The voice came from behind him. Jack turned around quickly to find Uriel standing behind him only two yards away. Sparrow wasn't with her though, which he found odd. Jack got up to face Uriel, suppressing all the emotions, hiding what he saw.

Uriel slowly approached him.

"Don't worry Jack, in time you'll be strong enough to use the Eye. But until then, I hear that you've decided to join our ranks." A smile formed in place of her normally serious expression and her silver eyes lit up. Jack simply replied with a nod. Uriel's smile widened.

"I'm glad you decided to do so. What changed your mind?" She walked past Jack and opened the box with the Eye inside. Possibly checking to make sure it was unharmed. Jack remembered what Sparrow told him about her mission.

"It was actually Sparrow who convinced me."

"Oh?"

"She told me about all the benefits, how I would get to help people, make a real difference in people's lives. I always wanted to be a doctor, so I figured the Vigilants would be the best place to use my power to heal." Jack had to embellish the story a bit if only to help Sparrow look good. But he owed it to Sparrow.

Uriel returned to him and paced around him. "A unique power, to be sure. It's very rare for an Immortal to have healing powers, but even more rare for someone like you to be able to control light and heal a large number of people all at once. An Immortal like you needs special attention, which is why you'll be reporting directly to me.

I'll train you, help you develop your abilities, and provide anything you need."

Jack was surprised by her eagerness. He was going to become Uriel's personal project. If he were to become close to her, then perhaps this would put him in the perfect position to stay close to the Eye. Their conversation was interrupted by a flutter of wings. The two of them looked over to see Sparrow entering the room. She approached Uriel and stopped just a few feet from her and knelt down.

"Lady Uriel, I was just looking for you."

"I'm aware Sparrow, and Jack has already told me the good news." She seemed happy to see Sparrow this time.

"He has?"

"Yes, and he informed me of your part in his decision. It seems you finally have your priorities in the right place."

Sparrow's face sunk in disbelief, probably not have expected such a good response. Uriel motioned for her to stand up, and as she did, the commander placed a hand on Sparrow's shoulder.

"You're to report to your previous post, I hereby grant you all your former rights and duties henceforth. Carry on."

The look on Sparrow's face was more than words could describe. It seemed that everything that had made her cold and unforgiving had simply melted away. She looked at Jack and he swore he could see her eyes welling up with tears of happiness. Sparrow didn't say anything else, she simply left her post. Jack looked back at Uriel, who had opened a drawer in her desk to retrieve something.

"Since you already have most of the Vigilant's uniform, you'll need this to complete your status as one of us." Uriel held out a white headband with a silver plate on the center for Jack to take. He happily tied it around his head. He was now a Vigilant.

19

Jack had been taken down the tower to its base. There, Lady Uriel took him to a training room. The room itself was very large, nearly the size of a basketball court. The walls seemed to be made from white marble. The floor looked like sand, but it was solid, un-moving. There were weapon racks like the ones he saw before along the walls. It was built to train a large group of recruits all at once, but now, there were only Jack and Uriel. Jack was to begin his healing training.

"Tell me, Jack, do you have any idea how you were able to use your healing power?"

Jack shook his head; he assumed it was just a fluke.

"Well, let's begin with some easy tasks." Uriel took a knife from off a rack and placed the blade on her free hand. As she pulled the blade down, it cut into her hand and a small amount of blood began to seep out. Jack cringed a little at the sight; he had seen blood before but hated imagining how it felt to have a knife cut into the skin. Uriel approached Jack and extended her hand to him.

"Place your hands over my wound, try to summon any kind of energy to heal it."

Jack did as she said and held his hands above hers. He tried to concentrate on making himself create that light again. He even kept reciting the same thought over and over: 'Heal, heal, heal, heal, heal,' but nothing happened.

Uriel tried to coach him through it. "Think back on that day, Jack. Try to feel what you felt when you first created that light."

Jack could barely remember that day. He remembered feeling deeply concerned, panicked, stressed. He tried to recreate those emotions. It still took some time and with each passing moment, more of Uriel's blood dripped onto the sand-like floor. Finally, he became stressed enough to summon a small amount of light from his hands. A wave of relief washed over him and the light faded. When Jack pulled back his hands, the cut was gone and the blood cleaned away. Uriel smiled and examined her hand, satisfied with the results.

"Good, now we're going to push things to the next level." She took several steps backward until she was several yards away. She raised the knife to her hand once more and cut another wound into her hand. She held it up for Jack to see.

"I want to see if we can get you to spread the light out further like you did in the square. Stay right where you are and heal my hand from this distance."

This made Jack much more nervous, he felt unsure of himself. Nonetheless, he placed his hands out in front of him, pointed to Uriel's hand and concentrated, trying to strengthen his energy. This time, it was easier to create the same amount of light he produced only a moment ago, but it remained small, the distance was much greater. He kept trying, creating small pulses of light, but none of them were large enough to reach Uriel's hand. Jack lowered his arms, feeling tired and ready to try again at a later time.

Uriel frowned. "Jack?"

"I'm sorry Lady Uriel, I think I just need a while to rest before I can pull this off."

"You have the power inside you, Jack. It comes from emotion, not strength. Try again."

"But I don't know how. I... I can't." Jack bent forward, feeling exhausted. He looked back up and saw that Uriel was holding the knife again. She brought it to her wrist this time and slashed it. Her arm started to bleed profusely onto the floor. Jack straightened up in shock and alarm. He tried to rush to her, but Uriel put her hand up to stop him.

"Don't you move, Jack! You stay right there and try again. If you can't heal me from where you're standing in the next few minutes, my blood will cover this floor and I'll be dead. The only way to save me is to spread your light far enough to reach me. Now do it!"

Jack's stress level was going through the roof now. He needed to help her immediately! He raised his hands again and focused as hard as he could, raising the light once more, but it continued to pulse in small bursts. The blood continued to spill onto the floor and Uriel was looking scared. Jack started to feel helpless, but he tried with every fiber of his being to make the light spread. He began to feel desperate and was on the verge of tears. At that moment, the light suddenly burst forth and engulfed the entire room in an amazing display. Even the people outside the tower watched in awe as its base lit up like a lantern.

The light faded and Jack dropped to his knees, feeling dizzy. He looked up, his vision blurred, as Uriel approached him and presented her arm to him. Jack could see that the cuts on both her hand and wrist were healed and the blood was gone. She helped him to his feet and Jack's vision cleared up.

"You did better than I expected, Jack. I'm very proud of your progress."

Although he was glad his mentor was okay, he couldn't help but feel upset. "You were willing to risk your life in the chance that I'd be able to make that happen? What were you thinking?"

Uriel smiled and brought her face close to his. She held his chin with her thumb and forefinger, "I'm an Angel, Jack. It'll take much more than that to kill me." She giggled and moved backward. She had bluffed! She was never in any real danger but acted as though she were to motivate Jack to feel exactly as he did that day at the Blacksmith's guild. Jack sighed, feeling like a fool.

"I think that's enough training for today. Oh, I forgot to ask. Do you have any questions for me about the Vigilants?"

Jack thought for a moment but had no questions. He did, however, want to inquire about something, "None come to mind at the moment, but if I could ask for a favor?"

"Tell me."

"One of my good friends is stuck in the mortal world right now. He's an Elemental named Tobias."

Uriel nodded, "I'll have one of my Watchers retrieve him, rest assured." She smiled and led him out of the tower. They walked without speaking to each other as they made their way to the portal. Uriel stopped him and placed her hands on his temples. Jack's initial surprise at this was replaced by shock as images started forming in his mind. He closed his eyes as Angelic script formed patterns and became more understandable.

"You'll be needing this, Jack. These are the combinations that will let you use the portal to and from White Gate, so you'll be able to return without needing an escort." Uriel removed her hands and when Jack opened his eyes, he felt like he could read the Angelic script. Eager to test his new knowledge, he approached the dials and formed a combination that he could swear read out as 'Forum.' As soon as he completed it, the portal opened with a blue burst of energy. He felt happy about having free access to White Gate now. Before he left, Uriel spoke to him once more.

"I expect you to report back as soon as your strength has recovered, understood?"

Jack bowed to her in respect, "Yes, Lady Uriel."

Uriel nodded in response and reached into her pocket. She pulled out a handful of gold and silver coins and handed them to Jack.

"Get yourself something to eat and do a little shopping. I think you deserve to get something you actually want for a change."

Jack smiled graciously and bowed once more, then turned and walked through the portal. His last thought before leaving was how he was going to feel later when he had to steal the Eye from his mentor.

20

Jack stepped out of the portal and back into the Forum. He opened his hand and examined the coins he had received from Uriel. Some were thicker than others and all were stamped with a large number and a ring of small circles along their edges. He noticed the thicker coins had larger numbers on them, so he assumed the numbers refer to the value of each coin--a simple but effective currency system.

He placed the coins in his pocket and decided to take a stroll through the square to look for some food. Once again, people gave way to him and bowed as he passed, to which he smiled in response. The square looked about the same as always, but there didn't seem to be any restaurants there. Jack kept looking around as he wandered down the streets, hoping his nose would catch something smelling good. He finally caught a whiff of some rather tasty-smelling meats. He followed the scent around a corner and discovered why he hadn't found any restaurants anywhere else.

In front of him was one long alley completely full of outdoor diners. Little shops completely open to the road like porches, small tables, and bar stools just as you walked inside. Many of them had huge bowls right on the counters where people could simply pay for a meal, then fill their plates with whatever they wanted to eat from these bowls. Chefs were concocting amazing meals right in front of the customers, chopping ingredients and throwing them right into cooking pots or frying them in hot pans.

As Jack walked down the alley, he felt excited. Jack had always been a fan of well-made food. Many of the shop owners beckoned Jack to come in and eat; his uniform probably suggested he had money to spend. He noticed each shop had a different cultural niche. Jack felt as though he could travel the whole world just by walking down this alley.

Jack finally stopped at an Egyptian restaurant. He discovered the smell of the delicious meats was coming from this one. A very eager host led him to what was apparently the best seat in the house. When Jack inquired about the specials, the host made a suggestion for the best meat platter they had. Jack paid the host with a silver coin of a small denomination.

What Jack got was a huge plate with an assortment of food ranging from smoked sausages stuffed with beef, lamb and pork, shawarma meat and pita bread, scrambled eggs, and diced tomato, and enough of it to feed three people. It was then that Jack realized if such a small amount of his money could pay for all of this, how much money had Lady Uriel really given him?

He happily began eating his meal. The sausages were so delicious, seasoned with herbs and spices he'd never tasted. As his stomach filled up, he heard a voice from the alley.

"Jack!"

He looked up and saw Tobias. He was OK. His friend ran up to him and greeted him with a warm hug.

"Am I glad to see you."

Jack was relieved to see he had made it back to the Forum. "How did you know I was here?"

Tobias sat down across from him. "I didn't. I just got back and wanted to eat. I walked by and just saw you here."

Jack pushed his platter towards his friend. "Help yourself, I'm about full anyway."

Tobias grabbed a pita and began to fill it with shawarma meat. "Man, have I got news for you."

"News for me?"

"Yeah, it's about Debbie. After you left, I followed her for a bit. She has an apartment not far from where she works. When she got there, I watched her pick up a photo of you and cry for about half an hour."

Jack felt bad, especially now, knowing she was in danger.

Tobias took a bite of his food, "Jack, I think this proves it. She really did see you." Jack's eyes widened. Did she know he was still alive? Or did she simply refuse to believe he was dead?

His thoughts were interrupted by the next bit of news.

"And then she was kidnapped!"

Jack already knew of this, but part of him still hoped it wasn't true. He hesitated before replying. "... I know."

His friend stopped eating for a moment. "What do you mean you know?"

Jack leaned in to whisper to him somberly, "I got a message from the man who took her. He wants the Eye in exchange for her life."

His friend leaned in as well and spoke in a softer tone, "What are you gonna do?"

"I'm going to steal it."

His friend's eyes went wide with disbelief, "How?"

"I don't know yet, I'm still working out the details."

Tobias nodded, finishing his food, speaking between chewing, "I heard about your enlistment; glad to finally have a friend in the service to hook me up," he smiled jokingly.

"Yeah, you'll also notice I no longer have a babysitter."

Tobias's face turned slightly shocked and looked around in disbelief, "Hey, you're right."

21

"It's not gonna be easy, Jack. White Gate is a fortress covered by Angels and Vigilants guarding nearly every inch of the place. On top of that, Uriel's chamber sits at the top of the east tower." The two of them were back at Jack's apartment where they had been discussing how best to get the Eye and save Debbie.

Jack spoke, "Not to mention, from what I could tell, Lady Uriel checks on the Eye every chance she gets. If it goes missing, it won't be long before she finds out." The two of them continued pacing back and forth, trying to come up with ideas. So far, the only thing they had come up with was the fact that the Eye was heavily guarded. Jack leaned against his dresser, finding it difficult to think of a plan when all he could really think about was Debbie trapped with that lunatic. Out of frustration, Jack kicked the dresser, which shook a bit, followed by a large thud on the floor.

"What was that?" Tobias turned around to look. The two of them examined the floor. It was the crystal orb that had held the shielding power, which Tobias won for Jack back at the arena. As Jack looked at the gift his friend gave him, an idea finally presented itself.

"Hey, there are more orbs like this, aren't there?"

"Power orbs? Yeah, lots of them. Why?"

"And are there some smaller than this one?"

"Well yeah, all kinds of shapes and sizes."

Jack smiled, "Where can we get them?"

"Oh jeez, most of them are gone. The only ones you can get are either extremely expensive or used in lieu of cash at the arena. Why? What are you planning?"

Jack thought a moment longer, then his smile widened, "I think I know how we can get the Eye out of White Gate."

22

Jack changed out of his uniform and back into his usual outfit with the red shirt and brown pants. He marched out into the streets with Tobias close behind him.

"This is crazy, Jack."

He kept walking towards the square, money in hand. The first thing he needed was a sword, and he knew a group of blacksmiths who would probably be more than willing to sell him one.

"Even if by some miracle your plan works, no one who has ever fought against the Dark Mistress of the arena has ever beaten her. There's gotta be another way!"

"Well, there isn't. You said so yourself that those orbs are extremely rare. If no one has beaten her, then it must mean she has dozens of them in her possession."

"Well yeah, but..." It was hard for Tobias to argue with his point.

Jack had reached the Blacksmith's guild. It seemed they had already finished repairs and were back to work at their craft. Jack saw the hot forge inside and felt a little uneasy at the idea of it exploding again. He was greeted by one of the blacksmiths, a short but burly man with short red hair and a beard. His skin was covered in sweat and soot. He wore a brown craftsman's outfit with a thick leather apron.

"Can I help you with--" the blacksmith's face changed to recognition, then shock, "It's you. You're the boys who saved us during the explosion."

Jack just nodded with a smile.

"Oh, you two saved a lot of lives that day, we're all very grateful for what you did. Although I don't believe I caught your names." The blacksmith's accent seemed to be a mixture of Irish with a little Amish.

"I'm Jack, this is Tobias."

"Ezekiel, but everyone calls me Zeke. I run the guild here, you see. If there's ever anything I can do here for you, don't hesitate to ask." Zeke seemed really sincere in his desire to help.

"Well, that's exactly why I'm here, Zeke. I need a sword."

"Well certainly, what kind?"

"Kind?" Jack never had any interest in weapons before today and he had no idea that there were different kinds of swords.

"Well, of course, son, you have your broadswords, your claymores, rapiers, scimitars, various Japanese-style swords, although we don't make any of those so I don't know why I mentioned them. You have your falchions, your--"

"Maybe if I just looked at a few?" Jack interrupted. He had only a day left to deliver the Eye to Vergil in exchange for Debbie's life after all.

"Oh, of course. I have a few specialty swords as well for placing on your walls and..."

Zeke just kept talking as he grabbed a few blades off the racks and laid them on the counter for Jack to examine. As he did, Jack picked up a few and tried a few practice swings. He knew nothing about sword fighting, Tobias had to show him how to use it properly. After a few tries, Jack found a sword he liked.

"I like how this one feels."

Zeke watched him swing it around a bit, "Ah, so you're a broadsword fella, huh? That's good, broadswords are pretty well balanced. Good in just about any situation." He began putting the swords back on the racks, save the one Jack had picked out.

"How much do I owe you?" Jack asked, satisfied with his choice.

"Oh, I'd say the first ones on the house, considerin' what you did for us." Zeke winked.

Jack bowed to him, "Much obliged. I guess I'll see

you again sometime, Zeke."

"One sec there, you'll need one of these." Zeke pulled a long piece of leather out from under a counter, "It's always a good idea to keep a sword in a scabbard while you're walking around town. 'Less you wanna make them think you're plannin' on startin' a fight."

Jack took the scabbard from Zeke and sheathed the sword inside it. "Again, thank you."

23

"Seriously, Jack. You're crazy if you do this!" Tobias was still trying to talk Jack out of his plan, but when it came right down to it, there really wasn't any other way. The two of them were heading out of town toward the warehouses. By then, Jack remembered how to navigate through the building to find the staircase that descended into the dark cave beneath the warehouse and into the arena. The familiar roar of the crowd inside began to fill the air. The oil lamps along the walls provided just enough light to see what was going on inside the cave. As usual, the crowd of drunk gamblers stood around the banister that hung over the cavern floor, giving them a top-view of all the action going on below them.

As the two of them reached the crowd, they were stopped by a bookie--a gentlemanly looking guy who was somewhat pudgy but could still pass for a bouncer watching the door at a bar.

"You lookin' to compete, young man?"

"Yeah, actually. How could you tell?" Jack was a bit surprised, was it that obvious?

The bookie pointed at Jack's sword, "Anyone who brings in a weapon is either lookin' for trouble or lookin' to compete. You don't look like trouble though, and you better not show me otherwise, understand?"

Jack nodded.

"Good, now we already got some matches goin', so you'll have to wait your turn." The bookie turned to look at his record book.

"Actually, I'm here to challenge Gabriella." At the mention of her name, the bookie's eyes widened and looked back at him. The room itself also got much quieter. All the banging and yelling that identified the arena faded away. Jack suddenly realized that everyone in the room within earshot of his request was looking at him. Anyone further than that found out through a string of whispers traveling among the crowd.

"You got a death wish, son?" The bookie's voice was condescending. It seemed that asking to fight the champion was like asking to play six rounds of Russian roulette by yourself. He didn't care though. He needed what the champion had and this was the fastest way to get it. Jack gave the bookie a look saying he was serious about his decision, at which the pudgy man shook his head, saying, "I hope you know what it is you're doin'. I can get you in soon, but you'll have to wait for the arranged matches to finish."

"Arranged matches?"

"Group of kids like you come in here, all competing for the champ's title, the finalist takes on the champ herself. It's about to happen now if you wanna watch, I'll put you in when it's over. At the very least, the crowd should get a kick out of seeing her back-to-back." That last sentence sent the crowd of spectators into a roar of cheers and laughter.

The two friends made their way to the banister. Jack remembered what his best friend told him about the Dark Mistress. Having witnessed her terrifying methods the first time he was here, he remembered the way she simply disappeared into the arena, the flashes of blue that appeared only when she reappeared long enough to let fly one of her legendary knives.

"Tobias, has anyone ever beaten her? Gabriella." Jack asked with a somber tone. It wasn't until now that Jack started having second thoughts about his plan. His friend replied with a simple shake of his head to say 'no.'

"Has anyone ever come close?"

Tobias opened his mouth, looking as though he remembered someone who did but hesitated. His face changed as he said, "No."

Jack's feelings didn't improve from that. "How is

that possible though? Everybody has some kind of weakness. I've seen enough movies to know that's true!" Jack half-joked. The spectators started to lean over the banister in excitement and blew whistles and catcalls. That could only mean one thing in this arena.

The door to the only apartment in the arena started to open--doors which led directly to the arena floor with only a short hallway in between. Out came Gabriella, wearing her legendary leather outfit: the leather corset with the dark leather pants that fitted her legs so well. A long row of throwing knives snaked around her waist and others were sheathed in different parts of her outfit. For all Jack knew, she could have had five more knives tucked away in her cleavage.

"If there's a way to beat her, we need to find it. Preferably before I go against her." Jack concluded.

"I'll tell you this much: if you ever manage, by some stroke of luck, to gain the upper hand, don't let down your guard for one second. She will not hesitate to take advantage of it." His friend told him matter-of-factly. Jack nodded when a thought suddenly occurred to him. He turned to face Tobias.

"How would you know that if no one's ever come close to beating her?"

Tobias looked surprised for a second and his voice seemed a bit defensive, "I don't, I just figured it was some good precautionary advice. That's all."

Jack didn't fully buy that, but he had no time to question him further. The arena champion's opponent had just arrived. He was much like the last person Jack saw challenge the Dark Mistress: athletic-looking, tall, carried a sword with him, and scared out of his wits. Jack barely noticed the opponent though. His mind was transfixed on Gabriella; he watched her like a hawk for any signs of any weakness. The opponent stood near the center of the arena, but she barely moved out from the darkness into the arena at all.

Merlin's Heir

The referee rang the bell, signaling the start of the match. As expected, Gabriella disappeared instantly. 'OK, this is it', Jack thought to himself. At first, there was only silence. The opponent held his sword firmly and was hunched, ready to either dodge or strike. Then it began, the first flash of blue, and before anyone could even see the knife, the opponent had been cut and was bleeding. He winced and moved away, looking for the source, but of course, there was no one there. More flashes of blue started to appear from every corner of the arena. Jack found it very difficult to keep an eye on her since she disappeared again before his eyes could even spot her. He ended up watching the whole match through his peripheral vision.

It wasn't long before the opponent dropped his sword and fell to his hands and knees in defeat, bloodied and shaking. The crowd cheered as Gabriella reappeared and stepped out into the center, taking in the cheers. She definitely loved the glory. Tobias poked Jack's side with his elbow. "Find any weaknesses?"

Jack shook his head, "No... everything she did was just too fast, she never slowed down or left any openings."

"New challenger!" the referee shouted, announcing Jack's turn to fight her. "New challenger!"

Jack groaned loudly and dropped his head to his hands that were now lying flat on the banister. How was he supposed to beat a warrior who was extremely fast and never showed herself until she struck, then disappeared again? Tobias patted his shoulder consolingly, "I told you, man. Nobody knows how her power works, so no one knows how to beat it. It's like she just disappears into the shadows..."

Jack understood that his friend was just trying to help, but he didn't want to hear it right now. It was just too cliché.

Or was it?

Jack's head was still down on his hands, but his eyes opened wide in revelation. He stood straight up and looked at his friend. He clutched Tobias's arms with both hands excitedly.

"That's it. Toby, you're a genius."

A burly man came from behind Jack and grabbed him by the arm, pulling him away from his friend who just stood there befuddled. As Jack was dragged away and led to the stairs descending into the ring, all he could do was shout once more: "You're a GENIUS!!"

24

The burly man stood behind Jack as he faced the stairs in front of him. Slowly, Jack descended, still unsure of what he could do. Although his idea seemed pretty sound, it didn't help him feel any more confident in what he was facing now. He stopped a moment and took a deep breath.

"You can do this, Jack. Just keep focused," he whispered to himself. He walked down the rest of the stairs with a bit more confidence. He had to do this for Debbie. The thought of her was the only thing that kept him strong. He finally reached the bottom floor and looked up, seeing all the spectators cheering, then seeing his friend, Tobias, scared for him. He looked back in front of him and saw Gabriella waiting for him. He felt a chill down his spine as he looked into her eyes.

She had red eyes like him and every other Immortal. Yet they were different somehow, almost darker. He reached the center of the room. Down here it seemed the roar from above wasn't quite as loud.

"I haven't seen you here before, handsome," her voice actually seemed rather feminine, but still had a dominating tone to it. Jack didn't give her a reply.

"The strong, silent type. I like that." She gave him a wink; she was toying with him already. "So what are you putting up for the fight? Is it even worth my time?"

Jack reached into his pocket and pulled out a satchel, opening it, "Is this worth your time?" Inside the satchel was all the money he had left from Lady Uriel. Surprisingly, it was enough to make Gabriella's eyebrows go up. It seemed she approved.

"And what are the terms if you win?" She placed her hands on her hips. Jack didn't give away any clue to what he wanted and simply said, "We'll discuss that later."

Gabriella giggled, "Well I suppose it doesn't matter anyway. You have yourself a bargain." As she finished her sentence, she started slowly stepping backward, away from Jack, and into the shadows. That seemingly innocent gesture confirmed Jack's suspicion, and he smirked. Jack drew his sword and stepped into the center of the ring, ready to fight. For a moment, it felt as though time had stopped. Jack and Gabriella had their eyes locked on each other. What felt like an eternity had passed before he finally heard the bell.

The moment it rang, Gabriella was gone. It shouldn't have been any surprise, but it didn't stop Jack's heart from racing from the shock. He looked around at first, waiting for her to make the first strike. He needed to feel the cut of a knife before he could do anything else. Another eternity passed. He could feel his heart pounding out of his chest. He never heard it coming, but he felt it when a sudden pain erupted in his cheek. Jack clutched his face, then examined his hand, a line of blood staining it. Another knife cut the side of his thigh.

Jack had had enough. He focused his energy and managed to create a small pulse of light in his free hand, waving it around like a spotlight. It didn't help at all, she was still nowhere to be found. Another knife grazed his arm, then another cut into his back. He used up all his strength just to stay standing. So far, he was faring no better than her other opponents. The stress built up in him so badly, but Jack was feeling more confident now. He concentrated on his desperation, and his body began to light up like a beacon. Jack's light began to spread, filling up the entire arena. He could feel his own wounds healing and his strength returning. The spectators were blinded by the amount of light shining from below. The light began to clear up and as Jack looked around, something caught his eye.

He could see Gabriella hunched next to the wall, blinded and holding a hand up to shield her eyes from the brilliant light. He had her at last! Before the light could fade away completely, he quickly ran towards her and with his free hand, grabbed the arm she held up to shield her eyes and flung her over his shoulder, flipping the champion onto her back with a thud and a groan. He kept hold of her wrist and held his sword point against her chest with the other hand. The light finally faded away completely and everyone could see the result of the fight. Jack expected cheers but heard only silence. Even Gabriella had opened her eyes and couldn't believe what she saw. The only thing that broke the silence was a random voice from the crowd above them, "Hey, my arm isn't broken anymore!"

The referee finally called out, "Winner!" which brought on a roar of clapping and cheers for Jack. Relieved, he released his grip from Gabriella. She quickly stood up and rubbed her wrist, glaring at him like a child who had just lost an argument. She turned her heels and marched off towards her apartment, calling out to him over her shoulder, "Well come on now!"

Jack followed her into the short hallway that led to her room. She stopped halfway through, grabbed Jack by the collar and pushed him against the wall.

"How did you do that? How the hell did you find me?" This must have been a first for her.

"I figured out your power, that's all." Jack felt pretty smug right now.

"Oh really? Care to enlighten me?" she spoke sarcastically, but Jack answered her anyway.

"You never set foot in the center of the room, not once you disappeared at least. My friend mentioned something about you and it all made sense. The way you 'disappeared into the shadows.' You quite literally meld into the darkness, don't you? The oil lamps topside light up the whole room, except for the walls under the banister, so that's the only place you can disappear, and that's why you always use throwing knives, isn't it? So I knew that if I could light up the darkness, then you'd have no place to hide."

She gave him a scornful look but she knew she had been beaten, fair and square. Gabriella released him and took a step back.

"Alright Sherlock, what is it you want from me then?"

Jack dusted himself off, "A power orb. And I understand you have many."

Gabriella scoffed haughtily at his request, "Is that all? Why didn't you just say so? You could have just bought one from me Mr. Moneybags." She turned and opened the door to her room. Jack just stood there for a moment dumbfounded. He never thought that was even an option! Shaking his head, feeling dumb, he followed her in. She shut the door behind him and Jack suddenly felt another chill go down his spine. This time, it was different.

He looked around Gabriella's living quarters. It was a studio apartment cut into the stone. To the left was a shelf with crates of food and alcohol. Next to that were some targets as well as empty bottles hanging from ropes dangling from the ceiling, likely used for target practice, broken glass shards scattered on the floor beneath them. To the right was her bed, not quite as nice as Jack's bed, but not what you would consider a peasant's bed either. On either side of the bed was a wooden closet with closed doors and a large workbench with tools scattered across the top. Large drawers sat beneath the flat top, and a bowl filled with coins sat off to the side. The room itself was lit by candles rather than oil lamps, and small bouquets of flowers hung upside-down from the ceiling, giving the room a floral scent.

Gabriella approached the workbench and pulled out one of the large drawers before standing next to it, leaning against the workbench, and crossed her arms.

"It's your pick."

Jack approached the open drawer and examined the contents. A large cloth lined the bottom of the drawer.

There must have been nearly two dozen power orbs inside, all of different colors and sizes. Inside each one was a picturesque representation of the gesture or movement needed to use the powers hidden inside. But Jack didn't need any of them.

"Do you have any empty orbs?"

Gabriella turned to watch him searching through them. Jack started moving around the orbs on top to see the orbs closer to the bottom.

"There's a few of them in there, but why would you--"

"Got it!" Jack interrupted. He held up the empty orb to the light. This one had no color or figures inside. It looked clear, just like the old power orb Tobias won for him, but this one was smaller, about the size of a tennis ball. It looked exactly like the Eye of Merlin. He stuffed the orb in his pocket.

"Thank you," Jack said cheerfully. He now had everything he needed. Jack headed for the door, but he was stopped by Gabriella, who grabbed his shoulder, turned him to face her, then shoved him back into the door with a crash that made the door vibrate. Jack groaned before looking at the woman with dark, crimson eyes. Her dark hair whipped around her shoulders in front of her.

"You came down here to my arena, challenged me, and made a fool out of me in front of everyone just so you could come in here for an EMPTY power orb?" Her hands still clutched his shirt as she moved in closer to him.

"Why did you really come down here? Huh? Did you just want to make a statement? Or is there a bigger picture you're not telling me?" She came even closer, her body started to press against Jack's, the spider tattoos on her cleavage looked as though they were ready to bite into his chest and poison him with their fangs.

"Or did you come in here, simply so you could be in my room, alone with me?" Her voice changed, it was less angry and now sounded more seductive. Her face moved closer to Jack's. He remained unmoving, his eyes never leaving Gabriella's, yet her eyes were wandering down towards his lips.

Her voice became a whisper, "No one has ever gotten me on my back without paying a price..." She moved in to kiss him, but Jack gave no reaction. Before their lips met, Gabriella felt his hesitation and stopped, looking into his eyes once more. She released her grip from his shirt and stepped back from him.

"She must really mean something to you," she said with a smile. Jack exhaled."I hope she's worth it. Catch you later, handsome." Gabriella gave him a wink just before he opened the door and left.

25

Jack walked right back into the arena, the crowd still cheering and whistling above him. He kept facing forward as he made a beeline for the stairs. As he reached the top, Tobias pushed through the crowd to meet him.

"You crazy son-of-a--, I can't believe you did it!!" Tobias practically jumped on him. Jack tried to make his way through the crowd as they continued to cheer and pat him on the back when he passed by them. Jack hurried through and made his way down the hall back up to the warehouse with Tobias close behind. Once he was back up the stairs, Jack stopped by a crate, leaning against it as he took a deep breath. This whole ordeal was more than he could take, but now he was one step closer to saving Debbie. He had about half a day left to deliver the Eye to Vergil now. Tobias had joined him next to the crate and nudged his shoulder.

"So?" his friend asked curiously.

"So what?"

"What's Gabriella like when she's not fighting?" He seemed pretty excited to know more.

"I'd rather not talk about it." Jack stood up straight again and made his way out, Tobias dogging right behind him.

"Why? What happened?" His friend seemed a bit concerned.

"I just went in there, got the orb, and came out."

"Oh come on! She had to have done more than that?"

The two of them had made it outside the warehouse. Jack stopped by the door, reached into his pocket, and pulled out the empty orb. He examined it for a while as Tobias stood next to him and examined it with him.

"Yup, that one should do the trick," Tobias

exclaimed approvingly.

Jack looked at his friend, "Only one thing left to do now." He looked at the orb once more before stuffing it back in his pocket and heading back into town. The two of them didn't say much during the few minutes it took to get back into town and into Jack's apartment. Once inside, Jack immediately went to his closet and pulled out his Vigilant uniform.

"Jack, I know I've said this a lot today, but there's gotta be another solution."

Jack took off his shirt. "There isn't one," his voice was low and he spoke as though he had made his final decision. Tobias turned around while Jack changed.

"We have an orb that looks just like the Eye, why not just give this one to Vergil instead?"

It was a good plan, but Jack didn't agree with him.

"He'll know if it's fake."

"You don't know that!"

"I do know that!" A feeling was haunting Jack.

"How do you know that exactly, Jack?"

"...I don't know, I just have this feeling as though he would know if it's the real thing or not. When he sent the message to me, it just felt like... he was familiar, somehow."

There was a pause, this was news to Tobias, "What do you mean by 'familiar'?"

Jack had just gotten his armor on over his white robes, "You're going to think I'm crazy for saying this, but when I felt his power, saw his face... it was like looking at myself. I mean... he looked nothing like me, but I felt this connection to him. You know what I mean?"

"You mean like you know him from somewhere?"

Jack grabbed his headband and tied it on his head, "Yeah, kind of. I'm pretty positive that I've never met him, but it feels like if I know the orb is fake, then he will too. And if he finds out, he'll kill Debbie."

Tobias turned around to see his friend, the Vigilant.

He had a very concerned look on his face. Jack knew that Tobias didn't like his plan, but he couldn't really stop Jack either. Tobias knew all too well about doing what you can to save those you love, no matter the cost. His friend approached Jack and gave him a hug, the way brothers hug. Tobias gave him one last pat on the shoulder before they headed out the door.

The journey to the portal was spent in silence, the fake orb was burning a hole under Jack's white robes, begging to be let out. As the two of them reached the steps to the portal to White Gate, they stopped and looked up to stare at it. Tobias turned to Jack, "Good luck in there. I'll be waiting here for you to get back." He extended his hand to him.

Jack took his outstretched hand and shook it once, but didn't let go, "Thank you."

"Of course, anytime."

"No, I mean it. Thank you for... everything. I'd probably still be wandering these streets

alone if it weren't for you."

Tobias didn't reply. He simply smiled and nodded. Jack traversed up the steps to the portal. He could still see the combination he needed in his mind. He turned the dials to what he could read spelled out 'White.' When the last dial clicked in place, the portal opened with the burst of blue. Jack took a deep breath, his hands getting sweaty, his heart racing. Resolved to see this through to the end, he stepped into the portal and took off to White Gate as the portal closed behind him.

26

White Gate seemed quiet when he arrived. A bit more quiet than usual. There were still Angels flying around, but not nearly as many as usual. Walking down the main path, there was almost nothing going on, no Vigilants anywhere. Jack made his way to the east tower, where Uriel's office was located. As he entered from the bottom floor, he wondered how he was going to reach the top floor. In the past, it was always either Uriel or Sparrow who flew him up and down the tower. It was then he wondered how the Vigilants normally got up and down the tower each day. He wandered through the many halls inside until he found a set of stairs leading up.

He climbed up several stories; the tower was so high from the outside and having to take the stairs all the way up left Jack feeling exhausted after a while. After nearly half an hour of climbing, Jack found that the stairs didn't go any higher. It was still quite a way up to Uriel's office. That was not something he wanted to find out right now. He explored the floor he was currently at and found that this floor looked similar to a library. There were maps on the walls and on tables. All of them were for locations Jack had never seen before. He had hoped to find another set of stairs, his time to find the Eye running low. Then he heard a familiar voice call out to him.

"Jack? What are you doing here?" It was Sparrow carrying a few scrolls under her arm.

She pointed to the headband on his head, "I see it's official now, congratulations." She smiled at him.

"Thanks. Actually, I was just trying to get to Lady Uriel's office up top, but it looks like the stairs stop here." He did his best to stay casual.

"Yeah, this floor is just for intelligence in the battle against the Abyssal Throne."

That name sounded familiar, Jack thought to himself. "I've heard that name before. What is the Abyssal Throne exactly?"

"Well... seeing as you're a Vigilant now, I can tell you that the Abyssal Throne is the realm ruled by The Morningstar. He was once a very important Angel here in White Gate, but he betrayed us. So the Creator had his wings cut and sentenced him to a desolate realm where nothing thrives. Ever since then, he's been amassing power and resources, trying to create an army greater than ours so he can invade. It's been a regular Cold War ever since."

That sounded very familiar to Jack. "So basically, it's hell."

Sparrow shrugged, "Pretty much. But remember that's only what you called it when you were alive." Jack had to remember that this was his new life now and nothing was how he remembered. But that thought was short-lived when he remembered his reason for being here.

"Can you get me to Lady Uriel's office, Sparrow? Just as a favor."

"I suppose, just wait here one second." Sparrow traveled to a window with another Angel near it. She passed the scrolls to him, "Make sure these get to the Riders."

'The Riders?' Jack thought. Yet another name he had no idea about. Once the Angel was gone, Sparrow wrapped her arms around Jack and started to fly up, ascending the tower. Jack was glad to see Sparrow again, knowing now that she was kinder than she had first appeared.

"Why don't the stairs go this high?" Jack asked.

"These levels are all quarters for the other Angels, so there's no need to have stairs up here."

"I see. Now, who are the Riders?" Jack was still eager to learn as much as possible.

"The Riders are warriors, all loyal to White Gate. They're the only reason the Abyssal Throne hasn't invaded us already."

"They're that strong?" Jack was impressed. He couldn't imagine a small group of warriors were enough to scare off the army of the underworld.

"Yeah, you might meet them one day, but not for a long time."

Jack was about to ask why, but they had just arrived at Uriel's chamber. Sparrow set him down on the floor. As they both looked around, it seemed that Uriel wasn't in at this time either.

"Well that's not surprising, she's rarely here anyway. Why did you need to come up here anyway?"

"Oh, she wanted me to report here as soon as possible."

Sparrow seemed a bit annoyed, "So she wasn't expecting you. OK, I'll see if I can find her." Jack imagined that she was taking time away from her work to help him. He appreciated it.

Sparrow flew off and descended the tower again. Jack was left all alone in her office now. There was an eerie silence to the room that disturbed Jack.

Without wasting time, he turned his attention to the wooden box on the desk. Jack reached into his robes and pulled out the substitute orb. Very slowly, he approached the desk and opened the box that held the Eye inside. Jack first held the second orb next to it, if only to ensure that the two orbs were identical. Satisfied that the orbs looked identical enough, Jack pulled out a strip of cloth and covered the Eye with it, so as not to touch it directly and suffer all the visions at once again. He took the Eye out of the box, wrapped it in the cloth and placed it in his robes, away from sight. He then placed the second orb in the box and closed the lid. He had done it, he had stolen the Eye of Merlin. All that remained was to get out of White Gate and find Vergil, then save Debbie. He was sweating and his limbs shook. This wasn't any normal theft, this was a theft from one of the strongest Angels in White Gate.

Jack stepped away from the desk and waited for

Sparrow and Uriel to return. He began to get impatient and paced back and forth. He tried to control his breathing to stay calm. Soon enough, both Lady Uriel and Sparrow appeared from the opening in the floor and landed inside the office. It was Uriel who spoke first.

"Jack, I wasn't expecting to see you here so soon."

Jack tried his best to keep his composure, "You asked me to report when I was feeling better, and I am."

"Are you sure? You don't look well, you're sweating pretty bad."

'Crap', he thought. He wasn't hiding his emotions very well.

"Well as things would have it, I'm actually in the middle of organizing an operation at the moment. I'm afraid I can't give you anymore training today, but perhaps tomorrow." As Uriel spoke, she walked past Jack to her desk. Her hand glided across the wooden box, which now holds the wrong orb. Jack's heart raced, knowing she was eventually going to check on the orb but hoped he was far away when she did. His heart nearly stopped when Uriel opened the box to look at the orb. It seemed as though she looked at it for almost an eternity before she finally closed the box and approached Jack, stopping just in front of him with a strange look. That was it, she knew and he had been caught. Then she spoke.

"I think it's better if you take one more day off, report to me tomorrow after the operation is done, understood?"

Jack's relief was immeasurable. He could feel pounds of weight falling off his shoulders. He tried his best not to let it show though, even if he was doing a bad job of it. Uriel looked towards Sparrow. "Sparrow, could you take him down before resuming your duties?"

She nodded her head, "Yes, Lady Uriel."

Jack moved towards the opening and Sparrow carried him down the tower once again.

"Jack, are you sure you're OK? You're acting kind

of strange," Sparrow asked, concerned.

"I'm fine, honestly," Jack spoke reassuringly, though to be truly honest, he'd feel better once he was out of White Gate. Rather than Sparrow taking him to the ground level of the tower, it seemed that she was taking him straight to the portal. Once they had arrived, Sparrow went ahead and activated the dials for him. Before she turned the last dial, she stopped and spoke to him.

"Jack, you know you can trust me, right?" She seemed very sincere, "If there's something you're not telling me, I can't help you. I know you're not okay, I can feel it. So I'm just gonna ask you this once: Is there something you're not telling me?"

Jack didn't know why, but it was the worst feeling in the world when he looked into her eyes and lied to her, "No."

Sparrow looked a bit sad, but she nodded and finally turned the last dial. As the portal opened up again, the two of them parted ways without even looking at each other.

27

A flood of euphoria swept over Jack like a tidal wave. As he emerged from the portal, the rush of endorphins made him fall to his knees, dizzy and breathing heavily. Tobias, who was sitting at the bottom of the steps, turned to see him and rushed up to help him to his feet. They descended the steps together, Tobias holding him up like he was injured.

"You have it?" Tobias spoke in a hushed tone.

Jack patted his robes in the spot where the Eye was hiding right beneath, "Right here." He could still feel the Eye vibrating, yearning to be held and to pass its knowledge to Jack. He stood up straight now, walking on his own. They stopped at a bench and sat for a moment. Jack felt exhausted, but it was almost over. All he had to do now was deliver the Eye.

"OK, so where are we supposed to meet this Vergil?" the fire dancer asked.

"I'm not sure where it is. The place looked like a warehouse, and I think I could smell the ocean." Jack remembered the vision he had received. He could still envision that place, the color of the floors and walls, the moisture in the air.

"So you don't know where this place is?"

"No, but now that I think about it, I believe I know how we're supposed to find him." Jack stood up and started heading outside the town once again. It was funny how he was becoming used to methods that were less than conventional to get the job done. Once again, they made their way to the warehouse with the entrance to the arena hidden inside.

"Why the arena again? There are no docks anywhere nearby," Tobias asked, confused.

"It's not the arena I'm looking for," Jack revealed.

They made their way down into the dark depths of the cave with the ever-familiar sound of cheering and the smell of booze in the air. They walked past the crowd, only a few of them looked at Jack with familiarity for his recent victory against the champion, Gabriella. Jack couldn't help but look down into the arena, wondering if she was fighting right now, or still in her apartment sulking. He tried to ignore his feelings for her as he made his way past the arena's banister and found the door to its storage room. He snuck inside and hurried Tobias in, hoping no one would notice them in there.

"Help me move this." Jack stepped to the large stack of shelves that hid the crevice that created a narrow path further into the rock. Tobias grabbed the shelves with him and the two of them opened the makeshift door. As soon as it was wide enough to fit through, Jack squeezed inside, followed by Tobias who dragged the shelves behind him once he was inside. Jack focused his power and used his light to see the path in front of him.

The path was as long as Jack remembered. The only sounds you could hear were the pebbles breaking away from the walls as their bodies brushed against them and falling to the bottom. The only other thing to break the silence was Tobias's voice, "What if something goes wrong?"

Jack wasn't sure how to answer, as he hadn't thought that far ahead. "I don't know, I'm just hoping that if all goes well, it won't come to that."

After a few more minutes of edging through the gap, they reached the large room in the cave with the Demon Gate in the center. The two of them approached the gate and looked at it for a few moments.

"This is it," Jack said, ready to face his foe.

"How is this gonna take us there if you've never been to this place?"

Jack bit his thumb, cutting into his skin and releasing a drop of blood, "It's like you said, this gate doesn't go to other portals. I just have to picture the place I'm going." Jack approached the side of the Demon Gate and thought hard about Vergil's message. The room he stood in and the colors of the floors and walls, the beams and the smell of salt water and fish. He had the image perfectly set in his mind as he pressed his thumb into the stony wood. As before, the moment his blood touched the cursed gate, it erupted in blue flames. The arcane symbols on the floor surrounding the gate began to glow gold under the blue light.

Tobias stood next to Jack in front of the open portal, "OK, let's get this over with."

Jack turned to him, "Tobias, I can't ask you to go with me. It's too dangerous."

"No way, man. We're in this together, to the end."

Jack couldn't accept it, but he knew there was only one way he was going to do this quickly and conceded, "Alright, together then."

Jack extended his hand and Tobias took it, shaking it. As Tobias smiled at him, Jack momentarily regretted taking advantage of this moment as he shoved his friend away from the portal and towards the wall of the cave. Before his friend could get up, Jack had already jumped through the portal, leaving his best friend behind as it closed. He only hoped that Tobias would understand.

28

There was only darkness at first. Jack stood in the silence, wondering if he had even made it through the portal. He let out some light and looked around, before knowing for sure he was in that warehouse. But where was Vergil? And Debbie? As he continued to look around, a ceiling light turned on at the far end of the warehouse. Jack whipped around in surprise, his eyes focusing on the figures in the distance. It was the man with the blue coat and round glasses on his face. That thief, Vergil. He held another figure by the arm, a bag over the figure's head. Jack slowly approached while reaching for the cloth under his robes and pulling it out.

"That's far enough, Jack," Vergil commanded. Jack stopped only a few yards away from him. Jack took a deep breath, then called out to him.

"Let me see her, I need to know that she's alive!"

Vergil smiled, "As you wish." He grabbed the sack and removed it from the figure's head.

At first, Jack could only see black hair, but as the woman raised her head, Jack could see it was Debbie. Her hair was disheveled from the sack and her make-up was smeared from crying. Debbie looked at Jack with disbelief, stunned speechless for only a few moments. Jack wanted to run to her, to embrace her but didn't want to provoke Vergil. He just looked at his fiance with tears in his red eyes, feeling helpless.

"Debbie!" he shouted to her.

"Jack! It's not possible... I buried you. I stood next to your mother and we buried you!"

Her voice sounded hurt. But Jack understood her feelings.

"I know, but... It's complicated. I tried to find you, I wanted to tell you everything. But I promise you, it's really me."

"That's enough for now..." Vergil placed the sack back over Debbie's head. All Debbie could do was sob and lower her head under the sack. Jack was close to tears himself, knowing she must have been terrified for her life right now.

"Now where's the Eye?" Vergil demanded. Jack held the satchel with the Eye inside and Vergil stared at it.

"Why do you want the Eye? You couldn't use it anyway," Jack reasoned. He had gone through so much trouble to get the Eye, he wanted to know why Vergil wanted it.

"That, right there," Vergil pointed to him, "is where you're wrong Jack. You see, I was a soldier in World War I. I gave my life to protect my brothers on the field. I awoke six months later and was brought to White Gate. I became a scholar, working for the Angels themselves. I learned about you and your heritage from Merlin. Out of curiosity, I traced your heritage back to make sure it was true and when I did, I learned about Merlin's second son. So I traced that son's line all the way down to the present and I was shocked to learn the truth."

Jack was surprised to learn this. He remembered hearing from Lady Uriel that Merlin had two sons, but hadn't considered that it would mean two family lines.

"The other son's family line," Vergil continued, "led to me..."

Jack's eyes went wide. Now, this whole ordeal made sense.

"You see Jack, I too, am Merlin's Heir. You inherited Merlin's ability to heal the wounded, and I inherited his mastery over the elements. I brought my findings to the Angels, but they disregarded me! Told me I was still just an Elemental and continued to focus on you!"

Jack pointed back at Vergil this time, "So you stole the Eye from them, knowing that your ability to use it would prove your heritage to Merlin."

"Exactly... and if not for that explosion in the square, I'd still have the Eye now! All the glory and recognition should have been mine, but they passed it over to you instead. To them, I was just a lowly servant!" Vergil removed the sack from Debbie's head once more. "Now, one more time. The Eye, for Debbie."

Jack hesitated only a moment, looking back into Debbie's eyes. He clutched the cloth in his hand, then tossed it into the air towards Vergil. The thief caught it with his free hand, then used his teeth to open the cloth to check the contents. The Eye shone under the ceiling light and Vergil smiled. He touched the crystal orb with his fingers and his body froze for a moment. He was using it to see that it was real. Satisfied, he removed his fingers and let the Eye slip back into the satchel.

"It seems that the situation has changed. I'm afraid I can't let your girlfriend go. It's time for me to go and if you follow me, I will kill her, and then I will kill you."

Jack was shocked, "That wasn't part of the deal!"

Vergil started to back away still clutching Debbie's arm, "As I said, the situation has changed. Deal with it!"

Jack looked at Debbie one last time, as Debbie looked back at him, her face changed. Suddenly, she acted, quickly shoving into Vergil and knocking him on the floor. The satchel fell out of his hand and bounced a short distance away from him. The next few seconds seemed as though they happened in slow motion. Debbie grabbed the satchel off the floor and flung it to

Jack. Jack caught the satchel and raced towards Debbie, the two of them running toward each other. Vergil screamed as he got to his feet.

"STUPID MORTAL!!" As he yelled, Vergil jutted out his hand and a frightening eruption of flames burst forth and struck Debbie just a few feet from Jack's arms. Jack's worst nightmare had come true. He could only watch as the love of his life was engulfed in flames, screaming. It was the same scream he heard each time Jack had touched the

Eye. It was as though he could hear all of those screams at once now. The fire burned so hotly that Debbie's body was incinerated into ashes within a few seconds.

Jack dropped to his knees in horror as Debbie's ashes laid scattered across the floor in front of him. Jack felt dead inside like he would never be happy again, never feel anything again. He failed her, despite how hard he had tried to save her. He could see Vergil stepping closer to him, furious. Jack suddenly felt a very deep fear of the man in blue. Jack scurried backward, trying to get away from him. Vergil shot a burst of flame towards Jack, just missing him. Scared, Jack could only hold up his arms in front of him, unleashing the purple shield that surrounded him like a hamster ball. Vergil angrily unleashed a fury of fire at him, but couldn't penetrate his shield. But it didn't stop him from trying, he knew Jack's shield would have to come down some time.

He screamed at Jack, "I WANT THE EYE!!" relentlessly trying to burn him. Jack was already starting to feel the shield's power getting weaker. He somehow knew his shield would only protect him for as long as it could withstand the damage. Jack was sweating profusely, frightened, weak, losing his will to fight. All seemed lost and Jack thought he was going to die again, but it was at that moment he heard a voice.

"Focus, Jack. All is not lost yet! Focus and say these words:
A hanc potestatem, involucro inimicus meus."

Jack was surprised by the voice, unsure of the source. He tried to listen for it again as he tried his best to hold up the shield.

"Come on, Jack! Focus!
A hanc potestatem, involucro inimicus meus.
Speak the words with me, Jack"

Jack focused as best he could, the shield felt as though it would break at any moment. He recited the words together with the voice:

"A hanc potestatem, involucro inimicus meus."
"A hanc potestatem, involucro inimicus meus."

Jack's shield lit up brightly and left Jack's body. It flew right into the flames and at Vergil, who yelled in surprise as the flames disappeared. When they both stood up, the reason became obvious. Rather than protect Jack, the hamster ball-like shield was encapsulating Vergil. The thief tried to punch through it, but it wouldn't break. He shot fire at it but caused no damage. No matter what Vergil did, the shield would not let him go. It had become his prison; he was trapped.

29

A large crash clamored throughout the warehouse, followed by several more. Large holes tore through the ceiling and doors of the building they were in, and Angels and Vigilants flooded in. All of them rushed in and secured the area. Several angels surrounded Vergil inside his new prison. As Jack looked around, he saw Sparrow and Lady Uriel enter the building. Uriel was shouting orders, demanding equipment and searches for any possible associates. Once the army of Vigilants had begun working, Uriel knelt next to Jack and placed a hand on his shoulder. Her touch was soft and caring.

"Jack, are you alright?" Her voice was gentle and sympathetic.

"Debbie... she's gone." Jack's voice was like a whisper.

"I know, Jack. I can never apologize enough for her loss."

"How did you know I was here?" He looked at his mentor.

"To tell you the truth, I knew all along about Vergil."

Jack stood up to face her, "You did? And you didn't tell me?"

"We didn't know how to find him. So I planned a sting operation to arrest him. I knew all along about his heritage from Merlin, but we didn't want to reveal anything until we had both you and Vergil at White Gate, for your own protection. It was obvious that Vergil was going to use you to take the Eye back, and I knew you would be resolved to do it, so I made sure you had enough money to arrange the theft at White Gate."

"So you knew that the orb I left in the box was fake?" Jack exclaimed.

"Yes, Jack. For this operation to work, I needed everyone to believe that the theft was real."

Jack took a step back, "Even me." Uriel nodded in reply.

"Then why didn't you get here sooner? Debbie would still be alive!" Jack shouted furiously.

Uriel exhaled with regret, "The plan was to wait until the exchange was done and Debbie was safe. Then we would move in and apprehend him and take back the Eye. We didn't think Debbie would do what she did. I'm so sorry, Jack."

Jack fell to his knees again. Debbie's ashes still lying in front of him. As he looked at them, he knew he owed it to Debbie to repay what she had done for him.

"I need a jar, a satchel, something!" Jack demanded.

Uriel pointed to one of the Vigilantes, who approached and gave Jack his satchel. Jack laid it on the ground and used his hand to sweep as much of Debbie's ashes into it as he could. Uriel decided to give him some space and left to attend to Vergil, ordering the Vigilants to tie up the prisoner and take him to White Gate. Vergil kept trying to escape the whole time.

Jack closed satchel and stood up. He knew the beach was only a few minutes away because he could still smell the salt water, but he was immediately stopped by Sparrow who looked rather upset. Her green eyes were welling up and her bottom lip twitched a bit.

"You lied to me, Jack," she said in a hurt tone.

"Sparrow, I... I had to..."

"I thought we could trust each other, I thought I was your friend. I could have helped you!" She seemed on the verge of tears, "But I guess I trusted you more than you trusted me. And in the end, we were both wrong." Sparrow picked up the Eye and stormed away, leaving the warehouse. The Eye would be returned to White Gate where it belongs. Jack felt horrible, as she really was the first friend he had since he became Immortal. She truly would have helped him if he had just spoken up. There was nothing to do now but walk to the beach.

Outside, the world looked much the same as it did when Jack had died. The sun had already set, the last traces of light were fading over the horizon and the sky was a very peaceful blue. He walked down the concrete road away from the pier and towards the road to the beach. Jack turned the corner past another warehouse and saw the beach at last. The first thing he felt was the warm ocean breeze that blew over him. The beach was at its closing hour, so there wasn't much of anyone left there. Before Jack's feet could touch the sand, he heard a voice calling out to him.

"Jack, wait." It was Uriel. She had flown to catch up with Jack. "I still need to take you back to the Forum."

Jack smiled, "I know, I just have something to do first."

Uriel noticed the satchel with Debbie's ashes inside. Knowing his intentions, she nodded to him, "I'll wait here," she said with an understanding kindness. Jack turned back toward the ocean and stepped onto the sand. He wondered what Debbie must be facing now. Knowing what happened when he died, he wondered if Debbie was now wandering through Purgatory as he did, or something else. Looking across the blue horizon in the half-light, he felt as though she were right next to him, staring at the same sky.

He reached the water and felt the tide kiss his feet, feeling sad from knowing that Debbie would never feel anything ever again. Jack opened the satchel and peered inside at Debbie's remains. He felt he had to say something.

"Debbie, you've been my best friend since we met in high school, and I've loved you since we graduated." He broke into tears as he spoke, using the same words he had said when he proposed. He couldn't bear to say anything more, remaining silent for a few moments as he tried his best to stop crying. He gently turned the satchel upside-down and watched as the ashes poured out and the wind carried her into the ocean. She had borne the pain of burying him, now he was doing the same for her.

Jack wiped the tears from his eyes and headed back to the road where Uriel was waiting for him. He stood in front of his mentor and nodded, keeping his head down. Uriel stepped towards him and embraced Jack, never speaking a word, but none needed to be said. As the hug ended, Jack looked up at Uriel, her pale blue eyes full of sympathy and regret.

"OK. I'm ready to go home," Jack said quietly. Uriel nodded, and wrapped her arms around him, carrying him back to the portal.

30

Tobias was pacing back and forth in front of the portal steps like a nervous wreck. He was worried about Jack and wouldn't leave until he knew Jack was okay. The portal burst open and Tobias reacted by rushing straight up the steps. He was a bit surprised to see Lady Uriel come through, but relieved to see that Jack was with her. The moment his friend saw Jack's eyes, he knew exactly what had happened.

"Will you stay with him?" Uriel asked Tobias. He replied with a nod and immediately wrapped his arm around Jack's shoulder.

Uriel turned to Jack. "I think it's best if we retract your enlistment to the Vigilants, at least for now. If you ever feel ready to re-enlist, or just need a friend, don't ever hesitate to find me."

Uriel was very kind to Jack. She seemed less like a commander now and more like the Angel that she was. Jack reached for his head and pulled off the headband, handing it to Uriel. For now, he was glad to be rid of it. Uriel left, re-activating the portal, and headed back to White Gate. Tobias stayed by Jack's side, walking him back to his apartment. Jack explained everything that had happened.

He told his friend about Vergil's real identity, the act of bravery from Debbie, the deception of White Gate to steal the Eye, and finally of spreading Debbie's ashes in the ocean. It was very dark outside and Jack lay in his bed, wanting to sleep. He thought about the way Debbie's skin felt, the look in her eyes telling him 'I love you,' as though he could will her into existence. He spent the whole night crying, with his friend sitting at the foot of his bed the whole time, never leaving his side.

The next morning, Jack woke up slowly. He had thought he might dream about Debbie, but he dreamed of nothing. He got up and looked around. Tobias was still there, standing up as he saw Jack get up.

"Hey buddy, how are you feeling?" his friend asked concerned.

"Not as bad as yesterday, I guess."

"That's good, I'm glad." Jack, glad to at least have a friend as good as Tobias, stood up and headed for the door.

"I think I'm just going to go for a walk."

"Do you want me to come with you?" Tobias asked.

"No, I'll be fine. But thanks... I'm glad you're my friend."

Tobias nodded and smiled, "Anytime, brother."

Jack left through the door and strolled down the streets, not knowing where he was going, letting his feet lead the way. As he walked into the square, he saw all the performers, many doing their amazing acts to entertain the Immortals. Jack smiled at their jubilation. He wandered past the blacksmiths and admired their steel, but left as soon as he saw Zeke walking his way.

Somehow, Jack ended up back in front of the portal, even though he was trying to avoid the thought of going anywhere else for a while. He couldn't help but look up the steps to the dials. Without realizing it, he started walking up the steps. As he reached the top, he felt the need to turn the dials. It didn't make sense to him, but Jack saw a combination he didn't know existed. He turned all the dials and suddenly realized that the combination he spelled out was 'Summer.'

Unexpectedly, the portal opened. The word actually led to a different realm he had never heard of. Something called to him though and he felt like he needed to enter this portal to find that something inside. Knowing better than to ignore feelings like this, Jack stepped through the portal. Upon reaching the other side, Jack was amazed to see the beauty of this realm.

The whole area was a vast valley of flowers and trees as far as the eye could see. The trees were filled with ripe fruit and the air was swimming with sweet scents. Jack felt as though this valley only knew everlasting peace. The only thing not naturally found here was a mausoleum just off in the distance. If Jack was meant to be here, he felt that the reason was there. He hiked over a small hill to reach the stone mausoleum. Though it had been made of mere stones and mortar, it was majestic enough to house a king inside.

Jack entered the stone sanctuary to find it well lit by the outside light. The large structure was entirely empty, save for a single stone sarcophagus with an effigy of an elderly man dressed in robes. On it was a broadsword, similar to the one Jack owned. But this one was different. He saw symbols emblazoned on the blade, like runes that almost formed letters. While he examined it closely, a voice spoke to him.

"Hello, Jack." The voice was kind, elderly, and somewhat familiar. Jack looked up to see a man standing next to him. He was tall with white hair that fell to his shoulders. Long gray robes covered his whole body. Jack realized he looked exactly like the effigy on the grave.

"Merlin?" Jack asked, somewhat in disbelief.

"Yes, Jack. I'm glad you could come see me. I know you've been through a lot lately." His voice still sounded very familiar. Then Jack realized where he heard his voice before.

"It was you, wasn't it? The voice I kept hearing in my head. You're the one who saved me when Vergil attacked me."

Merlin smiled, "That's right, I always knew you had great potential, but I thought a little extra guidance couldn't hurt."

Jack had so many questions for him. "What is this place?"

"This is the Summerland, a resting place for the greatest of magicians, like myself." He looked at his surroundings as he described them.

Merlin stepped towards the sword and ran his

fingers over the hilt, "I see you admire the sword."

As Jack examined it further, the runes on the blade seemed to glow.

"You see, Jack. I created this sword for King Arthur centuries ago. I blessed it so only those who followed a righteous path could lift it. It wasn't enough to lock it away in a stone. I had to make sure only a good man would have the ability to pull it out."

Jack finally noticed the runes on the blade really did seem to be letters: XCALIBUR.

"This is... Excalibur?"

Merlin turned to Jack once more, "Soon, you'll have need of this sword. I chose you because I knew you had a good heart, Jack. Vergil's need for power made him dangerous, and giving him this power would only put the world in more danger."

Merlin stepped closer to him and held Jack's arms, "You're my blood, Jack. And for that, I'll always love you like a son. Please, don't ever think badly of yourself."

Jack was at a loss for words, "Merlin, I..."

But his words were cut off when another figured appeared, rising from the ground like a demon. Before Jack could even make out the figure, a large claw sprung from Merlin's chest and appeared as if killing him. Merlin's hands slid off Jack's shoulders and fell. Merlin's spirit looked as though it were being sucked into the arm of the creature. The creature appeared to be an old man with wrinkled, pale skin. He wore black robes decorated by bones, fangs, and claws. He was bald with black eyes as dark as coal. He smiled and looked at Jack.

"Thank you, boy."

Jack stepped back in horror, "Who the hell are you? What did you do to Merlin?"

The dark figure spoke again with a hiss, "Merlin's spirit belongs to me now. I thank you for opening the portal and allowing me to enter. If you'd like to take his soul back, you can always come find it at the Boneyard. As for who I

am, you can call me the King of Bones. I await your visit."
And with that, the dark figure sunk back into the ground
and disappeared.

Shocked by what happened, Jack knew he had to do
something. He had to bring Merlin back. Jack owed him his
life and he was family, after all. Jack looked back at the
grave, with Excalibur resting on the hard stone. He
approached the sword and gripped the handle. Closing his
eyes and praying, he pulled on the sword. Excalibur came
away from the effigy with ease. It had chosen him to be its
bearer. Jack stood alone in that mausoleum with Excalibur
in hand. He swore he would use Excalibur to reclaim
Merlin's spirit.

To be continued...

ABOUT THE AUTHOR

Scott R Hylton began writing in 2013 when he entered the Next Best Fiction Author Contest hosted by the Hampton Roads Publishing house. Though he didn't win, this story did reach the top ten in the finals, out of 240 total entries. Scott spent his early-adult years serving in the U.S. Navy, seeing much of the world, and understanding different ways of living, thinking, and understanding, and he tries to apply these perspectives in his own writing.

www.ingramcontent.com/pod-product-compliance
Lightning Source LLC
Chambersburg PA
CBHW030207130726
47898CB00012B/910